An Island
in a Green Sea

AN
ISLAND
IN A
GREEN
SEA

Mabel Esther Allan

J. M. DENT AND SONS LIMITED

Printed in Great Britain by
Biddles Ltd, Guildford, Surrey
and bound at the
Aldine Press Letchworth Hertfordshire
for
J M Dent & Sons Limited
Aldine House Albemarle Street London

First published in Great Britain 1973
Reprinted 1974

ISBN 0 460 05886 X

Contents

AUTHOR'S NOTE

This is the story of a Hebridean childhood in the late 1920s. One of the islands may be faintly recognizable to anyone who has visited the Outer Isles of Scotland, but the story is fiction and all the characters are imaginary.

In the 1920s the Outer Isles were remote indeed. No one ever thought that there would be regular air services to the larger islands and that planes would land on the great white beach to the north of Barra. No one dreamed of—or had nightmares about—the rocket range that would be built on South Uist.

More than forty years have passed, but some of the problems remain the same. Many of the islands that were once populated are now deserted. Life grew too difficult on remote

St. Kilda, Soay and others. There is still a drift away from the islands owing to poor soil, lack of work and opportunity. There are better houses now for those who remain, and if the old "black houses" still exist at all, they are now barns or byres beside a more modern dwelling. Yet they were not wholly bad, as Mairi says in the story.

There are good schools on one or two of the bigger islands, but the problem is still much the same for young people on the smaller ones. They have to go away to get a proper education.

Before the Second World War many of the islands were owned by Englishmen, or, at the best, by Scotsmen from the mainland who were not greatly concerned with the troubles of the people. The Island of Rhum—one of the most beautiful from the sea—was at that time privately owned, and I believe the tenants were much-restricted. They had to have permission before they could have guests from the mainland, and the ordinary tourist found it difficult to land. Now the island is a nature reserve.

The Outer Isles are among the most beautiful places on earth, and it is sad that life has always been so hard there. They have produced—and probably are still producing—a wonderful race of men and women. Many of these people are now in Canada or the United States, and their children and grandchildren have never seen those "islands in a green sea." It is for them that I have written this book.

To avoid confusion it may be as well to explain that the islands are known by many names. The Outer Hebrides . . . the Outer Isles . . . the Western Isles. Sometimes, too, the Long Island, a collective name for the whole long chain.

MAIRI'S STORY

This morning as I went down the stairs on my way to work, I heard the lovely rippling chords of the "Glascreagh Love Lilt." I stopped at once, hardly breathing, for I had not heard that song in a long time. A moment later the words that Isobel had scribbled as she sat by the peat fire in our croft-house came to me clearly.

> By the green sea I wait for my love
> And he is long in coming;
> My heart cries with the gulls that
>   sweep the white shore.
> O my love! My love is long in coming!
> But the night comes and the wind cries
>   with the gulls
> And my heart is dark and wild as the sea.

The music came from the apartment below ours, where the girl was a music student. She had not been there long, but I knew her slightly. I had not known, however, that she was familiar with any of the songs of the Isles.

I am nineteen as I start this book, and I am working my way through college. At the moment it is the summer vacation, and I have a temporary job in an office, but I know I have to find time to write the story of my childhood. For the song awakened in me a great nostalgia for the Outer Hebrides, and I feel that I must live once more, if only in imagination, among the scents and sounds of the Isles.

Writing the story of my childhood and of the years until I was nearly fourteen, I shall recall so many things. The sobbing, tearing west wind beating around the croft-house and the warmth of Jean's arms as she sang the lullaby to which I nightly fell asleep, the fragrance of the bog myrtle among the *peat-hags* of Glen Gaoth, the gleam and sound and tang of Loch Alvadale, and the feel of wet wood under my hands as I pushed with all my strength beside Uilleam Angus until the *St. Bride* moved into the water. And a hundred other things, once familiar. They will all come back for a brief time as I tell my story. But it is Isobel's story, too, for I might not be where I am now if she had not come to live with us and had such a strong influence in my young life.

My name is Mairi Gilbride, and I was born of crofting parents on an island in the Outer Hebrides, those islands that are cut off from the mainland of Scotland by the wide waters of the Minch. All my childhood was spent on a croft at the head of the long, bleak valley that stretches from the south shore of Loch Alvadale to the rocks of the Sound of Glascreagh. It was aptly named Glen Gaoth—the Glen of the Wind—for the bitter north wind whistled down it, bringing the snow, and in summer the south wind brought the scents of bog myrtle and bell heather to our open door.

A stony path led up from the shore past the small *clachan,* serving us and our nearest neighbors, the Beaths. If we wanted to reach the township of Alvadale by road, it was a matter of several miles around the long arms of the loch, but by boat it took only minutes, and Uilleam Angus was always willing to take us if he wasn't busy.

It is all clear to me; the map of the island is painted on my mind. Down Glen Gaoth, a wide track led through bogland and moorland to the *clachan* of Arbhar on the Sound, but to reach it we had to scramble for some distance over difficult ground. By the time I was five I was jumping with the best, and I only occasionally browned my legs to the knees in the peaty water.

At Arbhar the glen became fertile and the heather gave place to very small fields. The track ended beyond the twenty or so low stone houses, on the tangle-covered rocks, where there were boats and drying nets.

Across the Sound was the island of Glascreagh, and my first real desire was to go there. I used to sit on Ulval, the hill in front of our house, and gaze down the glen to where the sea sparkled on summer days. I could see Glascreagh, Lunay, Tanneray, and many other little islands that were uninhabited and hardly more than rocks.

The men of Glascreagh came over to Glen Gaoth early every summer to cut the peats. For there was no peat at all on Glascreagh, and the winter fuel had to be dried and then carried across the Sound in the fishing boats.

I was always around when this was going on, and one day I found myself aboard *The Sacred Rose* actually crossing the Sound to Glascreagh. That day we saw seals on the rocks

3

that stood up, black and dangerous, close to the entrance of the little harbor. When I leaned far over the gunwale, so that my face almost touched the clear water, I could see fish and long dark clouds of wrack against the silver-white sand.

That was the first time I had an adventure, and it seemed a wonderful one to me. For I stayed the night with Mrs. MacRanald, who knew my mother, and it was the first time I had ever slept away from home. I was lonely and a little scared, but I heard one of the last of the great singers of the Isles crooning as she herded her cattle on the short grassland above a white beach.

The traditional songs were already being forgotten in the Isles, for the old folk were dying and the young people left for the cities. I am glad I heard that singing when I was six years old. It was worth the loneliness of going to bed a long way away from Jean and listening all night to the wind.

Jean was the most important person in my life until Isobel came and took her place in our household. She was four years older than I, and it was she who looked after me until I was eleven. I can see her now, sitting in the firelight, knitting busily. I can see her dark hair, straight and rather ragged about her shoulders, and the lines of her thin, pale face. In my memory of her she always has a cold and hungry look. Maybe we all had. I know that my mother was gaunt and pale also, but she had fine eyes.

Mother was always busy, always toiling in our sour half-acre of earth in the hope that the harvest would be sufficient to last us throughout the long winter. Often it must have been a bitter struggle, but I never remember actually being hungry. There were always oatcakes and porridge and usually potatoes and herrings.

My brother Neill was eight when I was born, and Martin

was ten. As well as mothering me, Jean also did her best for them, though she was so much younger. Most of her knitting was for Neill, who wore out his jerseys almost as quickly as she could produce them. He was a wild boy, dark and eager and never happy unless he was doing something vigorous and daring.

My father died when I was very young, so there we were; Mother, Jean, myself and the two boys. After a few years the old woman came to live with us . . . the *cailleach*. She was my father's grandmother. I never heard exactly how old she was, but she must have been nearly one hundred when she died.

She used to sit by the hearth all day, for her feet and hands were too crippled with rheumatism for her to move much. She drank tea. Oh, how she drank it! Pots of it, thick and black. And if she had no hard candies to suck, she was very unhappy. So when the tin was nearly empty, Neill would borrow a boat and cross the loch to the little store on the pier. Somehow we always found the money for the candy, but we never had any ourselves. The old woman never learned to speak a word of English, but it didn't matter to us, for we always spoke the Gaelic at home, though in school it was mainly English.

From the old woman I heard the old, strange stories that had been passed down from generation to generation. Stories of the Seal Folk, of the Blue Men, and of that mythical place the old folk believed to be beyond the setting sun . . . *Tir-nan-Og,* the Land of the Ever-Young. She knew the songs, too, though her voice was cracked and feeble.

Somehow there was room for us all in the croft-house. It was partitioned into three, the living room and two bed-rooms. There were three small windows set deep in the thick walls, one near the door and the other two at the back, looking out on the slopes of the glen.

The old "black houses" were not as bad as they sometimes sound. They were far more able to withstand the terrible gales that sweep the islands from September to March than the new houses they are starting to build now. They were warm and homey and not too thick with peat-reek; and the heavy thatching, held down by ropes and stones and renewed every summer, kept out the rain and cold.

My life went on peacefully until I was eleven. Then something happened that stirred me to the heart. I don't think I was ever sharply aware of things until I stood on Alvadale pier in a strong April wind and watched the departure of my two brothers for Canada.

Martin was twenty-one and Neill not quite nineteen when they emigrated to Alberta. They went with many other young men and a number of whole families, because they could no longer make a living in the Isles.

For weeks the discussions had gone on in the evenings, when we were all gathered around the fire. My mother sat huddled in her shawl, rocking herself a little in her pain, but always dry-eyed. The same scenes must have been enacted in hundreds of other island homes. The *cailleach* sucked her candy and blinked in the firelight. Her eyes were sometimes turned inward toward the past, and she muttered angrily: "Why must they go away from the land that bred them? There was always enough, though it was hard come by."

"Oh!" exclaimed Mother, in exasperation. "She was never the one for talking sense. She would always be telling her stories until the oatcakes burned or the cow was in the potato patch!" My mother was a practical woman. She had to be.

Food for us all was the dominating thought of her life.

Even I knew that things were getting worse and not better in the Isles.

The discussions went on. Mother could do the work of the croft and keep a roof over our heads, and Martin said. "Soon we will be able to send money home."

"But oh! I wish there were some other way!" Jean cried.

I knew she shed tears in secret, but in front of us all she was usually composed and gallant-eyed. But I—the forgotten watcher on the stool by my mother's skirts—saw the long, sad looks she cast at Neill, her favorite.

Neill wanted to go. He wanted to see the world and pit his enterprising mind against great odds. Heaven knows, the odds were great enough in the Isles, but I think he felt he would be really alive when he began to work one hundred and sixty acres of virgin land in a distant country, far away from the slow decay of home.

Martin was always the more solemn and steady of the two. It was with him that the decision lay, and in the end it was decided that they would take part in the mass emigration.

To me Martin and Neill were heroes. They were going across the sea in a great ship. They would see trains and huge buildings and places about which I had learned in school.

In some ways I envied them very much. I yearned to cross the Minch to Mallaig and see a railroad train. I would have given my strong new boots, of which I was so proud, or the coarse red jersey with the dangling pompons that had been Jean's gift to me on my birthday, for a trip across those miles of sea that separated us from the mainland. But I would have wanted to be sure I was coming back again pretty soon. Yet Martin and Neill were going all the way to Canada. I followed Martin around until he must have found my company

7

irksome, but he was kind and never complained.

I couldn't imagine a life without the sea for background, and I climbed to the summit of Ulval to consider the matter. Though it was April, there was a dusting of snow in the hollows, and the whole island was brown and grassless still. Only the flower of St. Bride, the dandelion, bloomed gaily in the crevasses between the stones.

But on the day of the emigration the snow had gone. It almost seemed as if summer had come. I remember I left my feet bare when I dressed and ran into the living room.

I think Mother and the boys had been up all night. They were packing when I went to bed, and then I had heard their solemn voices for hours. Once Mother's voice rang out, brave and clear, "Sad it is that our family is breaking up. But God and Our Lady must surely know what is best for us, and your father would have been proud to see the fine lads that you are."

Fresh peats were on the fire, and the kettle was beginning to boil when I ran in. Mother came from the byre, carrying a pail of milk.

Jean sanded the floor with the fine white sand we carried in sacks all the way from the western seaboard. I thought that she might cry any minute, and so I sat unhappily on the stone outside the door. I wasn't used to seeing Jean's lips pressed together and her thin, bony face white with sorrow.

But I wasn't really deeply sad at that point. I don't think I fully realized the tragedy of it all until a revealing moment on the pier. It was a brilliant morning; the sky was blue and we were going across the loch in Uilleam Angus's boat. There was sure to be a great gathering, too. It would all be interesting.

I think the *cailleach* and I were the only ones who enjoyed breakfast and the very early dinner. Neill was too excited, Martin too thoughtful, and Mother and Jean were far too upset to eat. The old woman wore her best shawl for the occasion and a big, old-fashioned pin that always fascinated me. It was made of wrought silver, and the pattern was a strange one of sea creatures entwined. It had belonged to her mother and the old woman never knew where it came from. She ate her herrings with enjoyment, wiping her plate as clean as she could with a piece of oatcake. She was so old, and I so young, that food was always a pleasure for us.

But suddenly her mood changed, and she grew morose and unhappy.

"I will not be understanding it at all!" she muttered. "It's just an excuse to be seeing the world." Then her old, wrinkled, yellow face grew thoughtful. "But they went before. ... Yes, a long time ago. And before that, even. But that was because they were driven."

"Oh!" exclaimed Neill impatiently. "And aren't we being driven now? Still, it does give us a chance to see the world."

Jean jumped up and ran behind the partition. I didn't think so then—Neill was a hero—but he must have been rather a thoughtless, selfish boy. He never hid the fact that he wanted to go away.

I thought how terrible it would be to go away from home for more than a night or two, and I stared at the round moon-faces of the plates on the dresser, at the black porridge pot on the hearth and the *cailleach*'s old carved chair. They were part of my everyday life.

Ruari, our golden brown collie, came from his bed under the bench and sat beside Martin, and for once no one shouted to him to go back.

Presently Jean returned, red-eyed but quite composed,

9

and soon afterward we went down to the shore. We left the old woman in her chair by the fire, muttering and praying to herself once the parting was over. She was angry because she couldn't see the great gathering on the pier, so we left a large pot of tea and a tin newly filled with candy as comforters.

Poor old woman! She felt their going sorely at the last, and Martin's eyes were wet. He knew, of course, that he would never see her again.

Martin walked with Mother, and neither of them spoke a word. He carried his luggage; an old leather portmanteau and a fine new suitcase bought at Mr. Campbell's store across the loch. It wasn't leather, but it was very shiny and clean.

I skipped behind them, wearing my red knitted jersey, and still barefoot because the day was so warm. I had no eyes for anyone but Martin, but I knew that Jean and Neill walked behind and I could hear Jean's soft, motherly voice.

Uilleam Angus was waiting for us down on the slippery, wrack-covered rocks. Many other families were coming from the *clachan,* a number of emigrants among them. There was a whole row of boats drawn up at the edge of the water. The loch had a look of summer, still and gleaming and holding the sharp blue of the sky.

Oh, it was thrilling and strange and half-frightening to be going across the loch on such an occasion. I sat with my bare feet in the water at the bottom of the boat and looked around me.

The clear sunlight fell on Jean's face, marking the sorrow in her eyes and the blue shadows above her cheekbones. She can't have been beautiful then, unless it was because of her gentle sadness, but to me she was lovely.

Across the loch I could see the buildings of Alvadale, dominated by the Church of Our Lady Star of the Sea. Ours was a mainly Roman Catholic island, like Barra, and there was another church on our side of the loch. Our church was very small, but I liked it best because it was on the rocks by the water.

As we drew nearer, I saw people in a great dark mass on the pier, and of course I had seen all along the big steamer that was to take the emigrants to the Clyde, where they would join a much larger ship.

Shouts, singing and the sound of bagpipes tuning up came to me across the water. There were more and more people pouring along the road . . . a road that was most often deserted and desolate.

I waited eagerly until we reached the pier, and I was the first to run up the steps.

THE EMIGRATION
AND AFTER

Men, women and children from all over the island were there. I clutched Jean's hand and stood very close to her as I watched the scene. There was old Mrs. Campbell and her son and daughter-in-law!

"Not many women would go overseas at *her* age," said Mother. "She must be well over seventy."

I saw John Leckie Donaldson, his wife and their two children, Mary and Cairistiona. Leaving Jean, I edged my way toward them. It suddenly hurt my pride a little that they should be going to Canada and I staying behind in Glen Gaoth. In fact I was torn in many ways as I watched the faces of the crowd. Yet I knew in my heart that I would never want to go away . . . not until I was grown-up and a different Mairi Gilbride.

Mary was only twelve, and she had all her possessions in a little carpetbag.

"I'm fearful of the ship," she confessed to me. "And then, when we reach Canada, there'll be a long journey in a train. And me never even in a motor car!"

"But you'll see things," I said.

"Oh, aye, but I'd sooner be staying here."

The talk was loud and eager, and there were snatches of song. Looking back, I admire the gallantry of that crowd, for many people in it must have been sad at heart.

At last the time had nearly come to say good-bye. The sunlight was almost hot, and there was a pungent smell of sunwarmed tweed. There was a sea tang, too, and the fragrance from the hills.

I moved around in the crowd, but I always went back to Jean. The air was filled with the sound of pipe music, with stirring marches and lilting songs. Up and down the pier marched one of the musicians, and up and down the deck of the steamer marched the other, both playing in time.

Most of the emigrants had gone on board, and Martin and Neill were among the last. The parting was terrible, and Mother's eyes followed them as they went up the gangplank. They looked splendid among the other emigrants; tall, well-made and handsome. I was convinced I would never see them again, and my throat contracted.

Gradually the mood of the crowd changed. Sadness crept in.

"Beannachd leat!" called many voices. It was the old Gaelic farewell. "Blessings go with you; may a straight path be before you; and a happy end to your journey."

Suddenly the weather changed, too. The wind rose and

blew coldly, beginning to whip the loch into uneasy waves. In the south and west, streamers of wild dark clouds trailed across the blue. The sun paled and lost its warmth.

And in this unexpected change of weather, the steamer slipped away from the pier. The sun still shone on the pale faces aboard. It gleamed on the waving handkerchiefs and on the long curve of the loch. How they cheered, those men and woman who would never see their island again. And how we cheered, we on the pier in the stiffening wind; cheered until our throats ached.

Across the water the sound of a lament drifted back, wild, sobbing, with all sorrow in it. The wind blew it over our heads, and it must have gone, plaintive and lost, across the moorland wastes.

Then it happened. Why it came to me, I don't know. I only know that for a moment, a flicker of time, I was standing in the heart of another crowd. I was seeing another, older ship slipping down the loch. Around me was the same feeling of sorrow, but the sunlight fell warm and heather-scented on the straining, desperate faces. I swear I smelled the bog myrtle on the wind. The clothes of the people around me were strange; the women's skirts were full about their feet, and every man was bearded.

For the brief moment that I stood in that crowd of the past, I felt in my heart an aching feeling of tragedy, far worse than anything I had experienced before. Then I was back with Jean, and her cold hand was clutching mine. Mother's shawl was drawn close over her head. She was not crying, but her face looked pinched and sharper than I had ever seen it.

We walked in silence to the waiting boat. All my excitement had gone. I felt scared and very cold, quite unable to understand that strange moment when I had been back in the past and filled with sorrow.

Our neighbor, Mrs. Beath, said something to Jean as they met above the stone steps. It sounded like, "And next it will be you, *caileag*!"

But Jean said nothing. She just smiled a little and turned to help Mother.

I did not know what Mrs. Beath had meant, but I was more than ever alarmed and scared.

It was good to see our familiar croft-house in front of us. The smoke from the fire was blowing across the hillside in blue-gray swirls. We were a desolate, silent little party; cold, hungry and glad to get indoors out of the wild afternoon.

The old woman had drunk her tea, eaten her candy and gone to sleep. There she was by the fire, crumpled in her chair. Ruari ran eagerly to meet us, sniffing and whining, missing the boys. The black oilskins were gone from the corner, and the two pairs of great boots from their place by the dresser. Everything was different.

"Well, they have gone!" said Mother, laying aside her shawl. "It's sad we all are, and the house feels empty. But we must comfort each other. Mairi, why will your face be screwed up like that?"

I shook my head, unable to explain. I was trying to puzzle out the meaning of my "vision," but, as I've said, my mother was a practical woman. I couldn't tell my experience to them all, as I sat on my stool by the fire.

I wanted to tell someone, for I thought I must have had "the sight" for a minute. I knew of such things. The old woman's tales were full of them, and, not so many months ago, Janet Beath had come knocking at our door on a moon-

15

lit night, panting and afraid.

"I was seeing my son Iain walking up the path from the shore with a weird light on his face and he in India!"

Several days later the news had come that Iain was dead . . . had died in India around the time his mother had seen him.

So when Jean and my mother went to put the cow in the byre, I drew nearer to the old woman and stumblingly told my story of the other crowd and the summer wind bringing the scent of bog myrtle.

She wasn't surprised. You couldn't have told her anything too strange to be believed. Yes, she said, that must have been the great emigration some time in the 1850s. It had been summer then, and a great crowd leaving.

The wind blew more fiercely around the house, and the smoke blew out in a stifling cloud. I was both triumphant and scared.

"But why was it me?" I asked. "Why should I be seeing a thing like that?"

She looked at me thoughtfully. "You're the sensitive one, little Mairi. It may be that you are having the 'sight.' My mother was the same."

"But it makes me afraid," I whispered.

The old woman was wise, and she said what I knew later was the right thing. "It is a great gift, Mairi, and it need not always be sorrowful. Some day it may even be a help to you. Remember that."

I was glad to creep into Jean's arms that night. It comforted me, but I could think of no way of comforting her. I knew that her sorrow went too deep for expression. Neill was gone, and it was unlikely that he would return.

As I lay there, something nagged at the back of my mind.

16

What could Mrs. Beath have meant when she said that Jean might be next?

"*You* will not be going away?" I asked, and Jean put her hand over my mouth in the darkness.

"Hush! We mustn't talk. Mother's tired."

"But I must know! Oh, Jean, you will not be going away to Canada, too?"

At that Jean gave a sad little gurgle of laughter.

"I go to Canada? To keep house for the boys, I suppose?"

"You would be doing it fine," I said, torn between pride in her and a great relief that my fears were groundless. "Fifteen is old ... quite old."

"If I were older I'd have gone," she whispered with a sigh. I knew she was thinking of the boys and so many of our friends on the sea in that fierce wind.

"It's wicked!" she went on, with such an angry jerk that I nearly fell out of the narrow bed. "Yes, it is, indeed! Why is it that the soil is so poor? Why is it that the trawlers come close inshore and spoil the fishing? Why does Scotland let so many of her men go overseas? Doesn't *anyone* care?"

I did not know the answer to those questions, so I said nothing, and Jean sank down with a weary sigh. I lay close to her, comforted by the warmth and companionship. Mother had said something about one of us having the boys' room now, but I didn't really want a bed to myself.

I lay wakeful for a long time, thinking of Martin and Neill and wondering if I ever should see them again. At last I slept.

The next morning, when I went down the path to school, all the talk was about the emigration, and we had a special lesson on Canada. It was a cold day, bleak and dull, with

17

periodic flurries of rain.

At twelve o'clock, when I was returning home, I saw Father Donald some way in front of me, evidently making for our house, unless he meant to visit the Beaths. He was a great favorite of mine, so I quickened my pace, though my stout, nailed boots slithered on the stony track. Father Donald's tall, straight figure paused for a moment outside our house, then he disappeared inside. I wondered what could be making him visit us so soon after yesterday, when he had seen and spoken with all of us.

I had to approach the open door slowly, because the hens were scattered all over the trodden, hardened mud, and I had to pick my way. They were used to me and didn't squawk.

Suddenly my mother's voice rang out:

"But Father, she's so young! Only fifteen. And it will be so soon after the boys."

I stood rooted there near the door. Ruari, who had been bounding to greet me from the far side of our small, bare field, paused and then came up to me quietly.

I didn't mean to listen—I didn't *want* to listen—but my feet wouldn't carry me out of earshot. Evidently none of them had seen me pass the window, and opposite the doorway was the wooden partition of our bedroom. What I heard, spoken in the father's familiar, kindly voice, seemed incredible . . . unbelievable. For he was urging that Jean go to a good situation in Glasgow. He said he knew it was good or he wouldn't suggest sending the *caileag* so far from home. But Jean would have to go eventually, for what could a young girl do in the Western Isles? The opportunity should not be missed.

"She might be getting a place at one of the big houses

18

when the English people come for the shooting," Mother said. But she knew, and I knew, too, that the chance of that was remote. For the grand English people brought their cars, their chauffeurs and all their servants with them. There was small hope for Jean.

As I stood there, I hated Father Donald fiercely. I and the other children had had many good times with him. He was young and merry and fond of us all. But when I heard him planning to send Jean away, I wanted to rush in and shout and hit him hard.

Just then the *cailleach,* who must have been crouching by the fire all this time, thumped her stick on the floor.

"*Eisd!* Fools that you are!" she cried.

Fancy calling Father Donald a fool! Only the old woman could have done it. She had small respect for anyone. "Would you have them all go away from the land—?"

I heard no more. I ran to Jean, whose blue pinafore I suddenly saw inside the byre. She was sweeping energetically, maybe trying to ease her pain in violent physical exertion.

She listened to my torrent of miserable, angry words, leaning on the broom, with her chin against her knuckles.

"Hush!" she cried. "Oh, Mairi, hush! You mustn't blame Father Donald, for indeed I asked him myself."

"You—You asked—?" I gaped at her.

"Yes, I did. Oh, Mairi, it will almost kill me to go away. But I think I *must* go."

I stared at her dumbly, and she went on:

"Always people have to go away. You know that. I can't stay here where there is no work and no money. And it may be years before Martin and Neill can send us some. So I thought if I went to Glasgow. . . . After all, it is not so very far."

But to both of us it was very far indeed; a great, almost unimaginable city, containing all the mysteries about which we had sometimes pondered. Express trains, street cars, huge department stores and, greatest wonder of all, movie houses.

Yet Jean could stand there in the low, uneven doorway of the byre, with her chin resting on the broom handle, and say it wasn't far!

"If I were in service in a big house, I could learn things," she went on. "And there'd be libraries and maybe classes at night. And I want so much to learn!"

If Jean wanted to go, then not even the old woman's fury would stop her. The future was a complete, frightening blank. I should be all alone with Mother and the *cailleach*.

I ran away across the field, wriggled under the wire fence, and was soon leaping with desperate energy from hummock to hummock. Jean called something about dinner and being late for afternoon school.

I went on leaping, somehow avoiding the half-hidden pools. Tears blinded me. I swept them away with the rough sleeve of my jersey. Pain, anger and absolute despair tore at my heart.

I stumbled often when I reached the uneven track. A flight of wild swans swept overhead, but I never even paused to count them. And yet I had always wanted to see seven wild swans, for the old woman had told me it was lucky, especially on a Tuesday.

I rushed past the cluster of small stone houses, hardly answering the friendly greetings. I suppose the kindly women, seeing my red eyes, understood. At any rate, they smiled and let me go.

Ahead were the rocks of the coast, a long black expanse of them, for the tide was out. The familiar shape of Glascreagh lay to the west, dim in the mist.

I hurried past the boats, stumbling over the nets, and on to the rocks. My eyes dimmed again, and though I rubbed them with my sleeve, the tears fell faster. The rocks were covered with wet yellow weed, treacherous even to the surest feet, and I was very nearly blind. Suddenly my boots slipped on a particularly succulent patch, my feet shot from under me, and I landed, dazed, hurt and still crying, in a cold sea pool.

I brushed my salty hand across my eyes, and they stung and burned. I heard someone scrambling over the rocks, and when the worst of the pain had passed, I expected to see one of the crofters from Arbhar. But it was no crofter who hauled me out of that pool, shivering and sobbing. It was a girl I had never seen before, an absolute stranger. And, in April at least, few strangers came to the Isles.

"You poor kid!" exclaimed a friendly, clipped voice, and very odd I thought it, even in the midst of my surprise and misery.

I said the first thing that came into my head. It was rather a disgrace to slip and fall on the wrack. I said, truculently and in English:

"I will not often be falling!"

I half-turned to run away, for I was very shy. But I was wet, my eyes hurt and I had cut the back of my leg. I could feel the warm blood mingling with the water.

"Of course you don't usually fall," said the girl cheerfully. "But it's hard to keep your feet on rocks when you're crying. Would you like me to bandage your leg? I have a clean handkerchief."

I nodded, snuffling back my tears, and then somehow it seemed too late to run away. I was so shy that I couldn't say a word, but I waited while she folded a white handkerchief and carefully tied it around my leg.

I want you to see Isobel as I saw her first on that gray, cold morning on the rocks of Arbhar. She seemed to come from another world. I was used to the faces of the Islesfolk, often handsome, often fine with character, but with hints of coarseness, hardship and weariness. Isobel was small and neat, small-boned, small-featured, except that her eyes were large and of the clearest gray. Her hair—soft, fine gold— was straight and smooth, but turned up at the ends. That morning it was swept back from her face by the wind. I noted with eager interest that she wore a yellow sweater, a coat and skirt of smooth, brownish tweed, and that her shoes were beautiful brown brogues, with mud and sand on the heels.

Suddenly she laughed and turned me around, shaking my skirt. She told me long afterward that I looked as if I had seen an apparition, and that was just how I felt. I had forgotten Jean and dinner and afternoon school.

A STRANGER
TO THE ISLES

Do you live here?" she asked, nodding toward the houses.

I shook my head. I was used enough to speaking English in school, but now, in my shyness and curiosity, it deserted me.

"Where then? You should run back home and put on some dry clothes."

"Up the glen," I said. "By the loch."

"Over the boggy ground?"

"Yes, and over the *fraoch*."

We were standing facing each other, and she was not very much taller than I. Suddenly she said, "My name is Isobel Darroch. Do you know of anyone this side of the loch who would let me live with them for a time? I came across from

Alvadale this morning to see, but I'm too shy to ask. I'm staying with Mrs. Alan MacDonald near the pier."

I gasped. Mrs. MacDonald lived in a splendid brick house, with two stories and a big garden. There was also a bathroom, an almost unheard-of luxury. How anyone could wish to exchange all that for a croft-house at Arbhar, I couldn't think. The only better place in Alvadale was the hotel.

Rapidly I ran through the different homes in my mind, but I couldn't think of one that would be likely to have room.

"There are the Beaths," I said. "Near us. But it is a little house. . . . Oh, very little and dark. A real 'black house,' for there's only a hole in the roof to let the smoke out. You would not be liking it at all!"

"Well, I'll come with you, anyway," said Isobel.

She took me by the arm, and we crossed the rocks together. To my surprise she was very sure-footed. Most of the visitors I had seen during the summer months shrieked and grasped at each other, wobbling at each step. Uilleam Angus laughed at them, though he didn't let them know. He was always courteous and helped them.

"If you can't think of anywhere else, I expect the Beaths' house would be all right," said Isobel, as we reached the track.

Though she had said she was shy, I don't think I understood. I didn't realize at all that she must feel "foreign" and strange in our familiar glen, with the sound of the Gaelic in her ears. I just thought that it was a funny thing that she should want to live there. And then I thought of something else.

"My brothers, Martin and Neill, went away yesterday, so there is their bed."

"You mean they've emigrated? I was there," said Isobel. "It nearly broke my heart."

"I was not seeing you."

"How could you, in that huge crowd? Was that why you were crying, you poor lass?"

"No. It was because of Jean," I muttered. "She is my sister and she is going to work in Glasgow. She *wants* to go to Glasgow!" And I told her the whole story. In the telling I felt less shy, because I felt she understood.

Then she told me that she came from England, but that her father's family had once, long ago, come from the Isles. She said that she had been with Mrs. MacDonald for three weeks, but that she couldn't learn the Gaelic there because everyone spoke English to her all the time.

"The old woman is not having any English," I said. I was startled by the idea that anyone wanted to learn the Gaelic. For I had seen the tourists nudge each other and laugh when they heard it, and in school we were made to speak English.

We crossed the peaty moorland one behind the other, with very little damage to Isobel's beautiful shoes. They were my chief anxiety. We passed close to the Beaths' house, and I saw Mrs. Beath's face in the window, staring curiously.

"We will go to my house first and be asking my mother if she'll have you," I said.

I suppose I looked at my home with new eyes because I was with an English stranger. I don't think I had ever really noticed the mud before, or the fact that the doorway was so low that people like Father Donald had to stoop to enter. I thought of the bed in the farthest partitioned space, and could not imagine Isobel lying in it.

Ruari came bounding toward us, then stopped at the sight of a stranger and barked shrilly, waving his tail. Jean appeared in the doorway, with Mother behind her. When she saw my companion, Jean disappeared again, and I knew she had gone to put the kettle on the fire.

In two minutes Isobel was sitting by the hearth in one of the best chairs, and Jean was fussing over my bandaged leg and wet garments. I knew at once that both Mother and Jean liked Isobel. There was something charming and dignified about her, and she seemed happy and at ease. They talked about the weather . . . how cold it was today and yet so lovely early yesterday. And about Mrs. MacDonald from near the pier.

And all the time I, bustled by Jean into my best dress while my skirt dried, champed with impatience. It didn't seem nearly so impossible that Isobel might live with us now that I saw her drinking tea and holding out her feet to the glowing peats, even though Mother was speaking very slowly and carefully and often chasing an English word for several seconds. Once, before she was married, my mother had lived in Glasgow for a time, but she had not spoken much English for many years.

The old woman, who had been having her afternoon sleep, had scented that she was missing something. She banged loudly with her stick on the partition, and Jean helped her to her chair by the fire. The *cailleach* gave a gracious greeting, for she always loved visitors, and she was disappointed when Jean explained that the stranger had "not the Gaelic." She sat sucking a butter drop, with her hands clasped in her black lap and her old blue eyes fixed on Isobel. The *cailleach* was always avid for anything new, and a visitor was a gift indeed! We saw so few people

26

throughout the long winter.

At last I could bear it no longer.

"She is wishing to live with us!" I burst out. "She is wanting to come this side of the loch and learn the Gaelic."

Mother, the soul of hospitality, looked startled. She glanced around the room and drew herself up slightly.

"But—you would be wishing to live *here*? It is very small, and the air is smoky, and we are poor folk and have not the grand things." She looked so proud that my heart stood still.

For a miracle was in the balance. There sat Isobel, half-smiling, eager and shy. Someone who was English—strange thing!—and who had no Gaelic. She had the wildest charm for me, and for the moment I had almost forgotten my sorrow over Jean.

"What is it?" demanded the old woman, staring at us fiercely. When she heard what it was, she nodded and said in her emphatic way: "Well, let the lass come. It's company she'll be. It's not so often we see a new face. And a pretty face at that."

But I think that Isobel herself had more to do with her acceptance than the old woman. She made us feel somehow, more by her manner than anything she said, that she would be happy with us, that the house was comfortable and warm and that she'd like to be with us. So at last it was fixed. Isobel herself broached the subject of payment. I don't think any of us had thought of it. She would pay a pound a week, if that would be enough.

"Enough?" Mother gasped. "But it will be far too much."

"Then I'll come in around ten days' time," said Isobel. "Mrs. MacDonald has been so kind to me that I can't leave her too quickly. And thank you very, very much."

We stood outside the door to watch her walk down to the

27

loch. The mist was thickening, and a fine rain was falling.

"Come away in now and have something to eat," said Mother. "A fine thing it was, Mairi, you running away and missing school. And Jean crying, and the old woman saying we are all fools."

And then I remembered that Jean was to go away.

"Jean shan't go!" I wailed, starting to cry again. "Oh, you must not be letting her go! What should I do without Jean?"

"Stop behaving like a baby, Mairi!" Mother said, with such unusual sharpness that I sniffed back my tears and stared at her in hurt astonishment. "You're eleven, and it will be high time that you behaved as if you were. No doubt it will be all our faults. You are the youngest, and Jean and the boys were always making a pet of you. But the boys are gone, and Jean may soon be gone also. You must be helping me."

"Mairi is right!" the old woman cried. "Jean will not be going away. I say she will be staying here to help us all."

Jean, who had listened to all this in silence, drew a shawl around her head and shoulders and ran out into the rain. We saw her pass the window, her face hidden in the gray folds.

"Now see what you have been doing, the pair of you!" said Mother, and disappeared behind the partition.

For days almost the only subject of conversation in the *clachan* was the emigration, but at home we had something else to discuss. Hour after hour we talked; hour after hour the old woman and I said that Jean should not go to Glasgow; Mother looked grave and sad but unwillingly approving; and Jean stuck firmly to her intention to go away and "learn."

I knew that she was torn between her love of the island and home and her longing to earn money and help us, as the boys meant to do. Mother could manage the sowing and harvesting, with me to help her, and Allan Beath had promised Martin that he would cut our peats and help us to stack them. With Isobel's money coming in regularly, we might be able to save a few pounds against a bad winter.

One of the things we had to budget for was, of course, the rent. We paid rent to the owner of the island, Lord Carlow. Lord Carlow was hardly ever there, but there was a "factor," another word for business manager, who looked after affairs. The factor was always very quick to collect money from the tenants.

I didn't cry again, for Mother's harsh words had impressed me, but my heart was heavy with rebellion and sorrow. And in the end it was agreed that Father Donald should write to Glasgow saying that Jean would go. In a day or two a telegram arrived to say that she would be expected on May third.

I think only I fully realized how she shrank from the change. We sat together on the summit of Ulval one fine, warm day, looking across the blue-green waters of the Minch to the invisible mainland of Scotland. We talked of Glasgow, trying to picture it from our incomplete knowledge. There were many things that Jean was eager to see, and they would compensate a little for the tremendous bravery of the step she was taking. But I knew that nothing could ever really make up for the loss of the familiar sights and sounds that had always been part of her life.

I think the thought of Isobel made Jean's choice harder. She confessed that she would have liked to be with her, to hear her talk and watch her expressive face. And, looking back, I believe that Jean might have learned as much from Isobel—though maybe different things—as she did in Glasgow.

We all took a great deal of trouble to make the house clean and bright for Isobel's arrival. The windows were cleaned and the curtains washed, the chairs and the old wooden dresser were polished until they shone. I found a handful of the flowers of St. Bride and put them in an old blue vase.

At school I announced that we were having someone to live with us, someone from England who was beautiful . . . like a Norse princess, I added, remembering the old woman's stories.

I had a ring of curious faces around me. "She's coming soon," I said. "Uilleam Angus will fetch her from Mrs. Alan MacDonald's."

"Then it's she who has written a book. Mrs. Campbell was saying so to Mother in the store," said a girl called Muireall.

"A book?" I was very much startled. There was awe and respect on the faces in front of me, and I felt a sudden sense of glory. "What kind of book would it be?"

"Just a book, Mrs. Campbell was saying."

When I returned home I poured out the news, but Mother and even Jean looked unbelieving.

"She's very young," said Mother, shaking her head. "Twenty or twenty-one, maybe. It's very learned you have to be, like Father Donald, before you write books."

I thought of Isobel's soft, turned-up golden hair and her wide gray eyes and agreed unwillingly that perhaps it wasn't true. We valued book-learning so very greatly. We knew of young men, and girls as well, who had starved themselves for the sake of studying. I think we found it hard to connect any kind of cleverness with well-cut tweeds and good leather shoes. If Isobel had been pale and shabby, we would have believed it more easily.

In spite of my excitement, I had not forgotten Jean's imminent departure. I went around with an ache in my heart, and sometimes I went down to the little church on the shore of the loch and prayed fervently that Our Lady would let her stay, after all.

Jean sewed a great deal during those last days. Her fingers, skilled at knitting but not so much at home with the needle, were struggling to make the neat print dresses she knew she would need. There was a black dress for afternoons, too, and white aprons.

They were strange days before Isobel came, sad and yet exciting as well. I believe the *cailleach* enjoyed them in her own way, for she liked to have cause for grumbling. Mother must have suffered more than any of us, but she never said a word. Sometimes I saw her watching Jean with sorrow in her eyes, and at other times she brooded in front of the loom.

The days that followed the emigration alternated between almost summer heat and wild rain and mist. At night the wind usually rose, and I think we were all haunted by thoughts of those on the sea. We missed the thumping of the boys' boots and the sound of Neill's laughter and powerful bursts of song. We all watched for the mail, though we knew perfectly well that, once we had received farewell letters from Glasgow, there would be no more news for a time.

I went down to the shore to meet Isobel through sheets of gray, slanting rain that hid the loch and the high line of hills beyond. She had sent a message across the water to say when she was coming, but I had doubts that she would arrive in such weather. The path was almost a river, and I splashed along it barefoot.

The *cailleach* had been sure that she would come.

"That lassie will not be fearing a wee bit of rain," she had said. "She is the brave one."

I battled my way through the "wee bit of rain" and the high wind to the *clachan* and the wrack-strewn rocks. I passed Uilleam Angus's house, and he did not seem to be around. His boat was not drawn up at the water's edge, either. So he must surely have gone to fetch Isobel. She would be certain to come.

The rain poured down my cheeks, stung my eyes and sluiced inside my waterproof cape. It had once belonged to Neill and was much too large for me. I stood in the shelter of a bank, straining my eyes to see across the loch and shivering with cold and excitement. We had not seen Isobel since the day I had met her in Arbhar, and one side of my mind was not sure that she was real.

I watched a great black-backed gull beating its way against the wind, and when I turned toward the water again, a boat was approaching slowly out of the mist and the driving rain. At first I couldn't see if there was a passenger, for Uilleam Angus's broad back was in the way. Then the boat swung around as it drew inshore, and I saw Isobel waving and smiling. She was clad in black oilskins, and rain and spray were pouring down her face.

I waved back and waded into the water over the treacherous rocks.

"Go back, *caileag*!" Uilleam Angus called to me. "It's swept away you'll be!" But I had caught the gunwale with my cold hands and was helping to haul the boat in.

Isobel jumped out, unafraid of the slippery rocks, and Uilleam Angus handed her a small suitcase. She had a larger suitcase as well, which he said he would carry up for her. I thought he must have admired her fearless jump, for usually he was ready enough to return to his fire and his pipe.

"I was thinking you might not come," I said. "And Jean said Uilleam Angus would not be crossing the loch in this weather."

Uilleam Angus gave me a slap on the back that made me stagger into a pool.

"There's no weather would be keeping me from the other side if I was wanting to cross, as Jean ought to be knowing. And I was wishing to do some business at the bank."

"Luckily for me!" said Isobel.

"The *cailleach* said you would come," I told Isobel. "She said you were the brave one."

At that moment the gale sent my yellow sou'wester clean off my head. It hung on my shoulders, held by the strings, and before Isobel could help me to put it on again, my dark curls were soaked and flattened by the downpour. We all laughed, and I began to feel more at ease.

As we passed the houses of the *clachan,* several people looked out to smile and give our guest a warm greeting. Everyone had heard that she was coming, of course. I think now that Hebridean people are a strange mixture. They welcome visitors, even complete strangers, with gladness and eager hospitality, and yet it takes a long time for them to accept and trust "foreigners." And Isobel was very definitely foreign to us all.

They were doubtful; they had shaken their heads for ten days over the thought of the fine English girl who wished to take a place in the community. And yet they welcomed her with smiling greetings that were entirely genuine.

The path from the *clachan* really was a river by that time,

33

and I was glad that Isobel was wearing rubber boots. There was a sea of mud outside our house, churned up recently, I could see, by the passing of the cow. The hens were making a great noise in the doorway. Jean, who must have been watching for us, flapped with her apron and they scattered.

There was no embarrassment about that arrival. Mother immediately began to help Isobel out of her dripping oil-skins. Off came her boots, and she was bustled in stockinged feet behind the partition. Uilleam Angus, oilskins and all, settled himself by the fire, Ruari was sent to his bed under the bench and Jean lifted the kettle and made a great pot of tea.

"What did I tell you?" triumphed the old woman, as I shed my wet outer garments and dried my face and hair with a rough towel.

"You should have been seeing her jumping from the boat," I answered.

"She certainly is a brave lass," said Mother, returning from behind the partition.

So we all approved of Isobel before we really knew her at all. Even Uilleam Angus, sour old fisherman though he was. He would never have sat by our fire instead of going straight home if he had not liked her.

When Isobel came back into the living room, she was dry and much warmer, though her hair still looked tangled and damp. She wore a russet sweater and the skirt she had worn when I first met her.

Jean brought out one of the best chairs for her and placed it close to the hearth. I sat on my stool as usual, and I think Isobel must have envied me. We were very proud of those chairs, though we hardly ever used them ourselves. They were too uncomfortable, though we never admitted it.

Within a week or two Isobel had bought herself a stool; a dear little three-cornered one, with twisted legs. But that first afternoon we were very proper. We were terribly shy of Isobel, except for the old woman, who was bursting with curiosity. She never took her eyes off our guest. She only drank half a cup of tea because she was concentrating so eagerly on our talk. Unable to speak English, she could understand a word here and there. She sat forward in her chair, her crippled hands gripping the arms, her eyes nearly starting out of her head. The firelight glittered on her strange pin, which she wore for the occasion. It took a death, an emigration or a distinguished visitor to make her remove it from the small box where she kept it embedded in wool.

Presently Uilleam Angus went home, and I washed the cups and saucers while Mother went away to milk the cow. Isobel insisted on helping me, and when Mother came back she was angry with me. What, she asked, were things coming to? Fancy letting a guest help with the work!

Isobel hesitated for a moment, then said in her strange English that we all found rather hard to understand, "But I can't live here and not help, Mrs. Gilbride. I couldn't sit by the fire and let Jean and Mairi do all the work."

Mother smiled a little at her anxious, pleading face and repeated that it wasn't right for a guest to work in the house. Isobel said no more, but her face was thoughtful as we put the dishes away.

JEAN'S
LAST DAYS

Then Jean, who had been feeding the hens, took out her sewing and bent over it in the firelight. Little enough daylight came in at the best of times, and that afternoon the living room was very shadowy. Mother picked up the sock that she was knitting for Neill, and I the one I had started for Martin. The old woman rattled her candy tin and took out a butter drop.

Isobel looked around at us all, then said to Jean:

"Perhaps I could help?"

Jean's anxious face brightened at once.

"Oh, I would be so grateful! There are three print dresses I must have, and a black dress and aprons. We were buying the material over at the store. It isn't very good, but it was the best we could afford."

In a few minutes Isobel was at the table cutting out the black dress. She wielded the scissors skillfully and was soon sitting down to sew up the first seams. Jean, anxious to add to her limited knowledge, asked if she had been to Glasgow.

Isobel nodded, and we all waited eagerly. We had met a number of people who had been there, including, of course, Mother long ago, but no one had ever given us a real, living picture of what the city was like now.

Isobel sewed rapidly as she talked, her hair falling forward like Jean's and partly hiding her face. She told us that she had stayed with her Uncle George for several weeks during the winter, and he lived just outside Glasgow. We hung on her words as she talked about the Cathedral, the Art Gallery and the great stores and hotels. She described the main streets and the railroad stations so vividly that I, at least, could almost see them.

"Oh, wait!" Jean cried, after a time. "The old woman can't understand. Please let me tell her."

So there was a pause in Isobel's talk while Jean explained in the Gaelic. The old woman nodded and smiled, very interested. She had never left the island in her whole life.

We had been brought up to be polite and never ask personal questions, but I was aching to hear about England and Isobel's home.

"Now tell us about England, please!" I begged. "Tell us *all* about England and the place where you live."

"Mairi!" Mother cried, frowning at me, but Isobel didn't seem annoyed.

"All about England, Mairi? That's a tall order," she said, smiling.

"She couldn't. England is so big," Jean remarked.

37

"Yes," I agreed. "There will be London, for one thing. That would take a long time to tell about."

"It would," said Isobel. "Think how many books people have written about London."

"Mrs. Campbell was telling Mrs. MacKay in the *clachan* here that you will have written a book," said I. Then even Jean frowned at me, and Mother looked shocked and reproachful. But to my intense surprise Isobel answered cheerfully, "Oh, but it's only a little one. It's about Gloucestershire."

"A real book?" I looked around and picked up my own arithmetic book, left on the dresser. "Like this? Printed?"

"Yes, printed, but not very like that. It has photographs and little drawings in it as well as writing."

We all looked at her in awe, and she blushed and moved a little on the high, uncomfortable chair.

"Please tell us about—about Gloucestershire, did you say?" Jean said shyly. "Is it a place in England?"

"There are trees in England," I announced.

"We've never seen a tree," Jean explained.

Isobel never looked surprised. She began to talk again, painting us a word picture of an incredibly fertile and luxuriant place. She had a great power over words. She knew how to use them—simply, never lavishly—so that one saw a complete scene.

She made us see the Cotswold villages lying below the curving uplands, where sometimes the bare earth was bright brown, but at other times the great fields were yellow with oats and barley. The patches of growing oats we knew were very tiny, sometimes not much bigger than our own living-room table.

She talked about the golden stone of the houses, and of

huge manor houses that were hundreds of years old and so beautiful. She made us see, we who had only known stunted shrubs, the intense green of a larch wood in spring and the heavenly white froth of blossoms in a cherry orchard.

Twilight began to fall early. Mother rose, drew the curtains and lit the lamp. The soft glow fell on Isobel's face. I learned to watch it that day, and for years her ever-changing expressions and her aliveness never ceased to delight me.

Isobel stopped abruptly and looked up at us. I longed to ask a question; it burned on my tongue. It had to be asked! "But if England is like that, why have you come here?"

Mother was shocked again. "That will be enough, Mairi!" she said sharply. "And indeed it's time we had something to eat. Isobel will be hungry and tired of talking." She began to bustle around, preparing potatoes and herrings.

Isobel laughed. "It wasn't rude of her to ask, Mrs. Gilbride. It's very easy to answer. I feel I belong here in a way. We aren't a real Gloucestershire family. My great-grandfather came from the Isles and my great-grandmother from the mainland, near Inverness. And my grandfather on my father's side lived in the Highlands for most of his life. I want to get to know Scotland, particularly the Isles. I want to get to know it really well and feel I *do* belong."

I think we were all conscious of the bleakness and barrenness of our island. We felt just then that we could offer nothing that would really compensate her for the loss of uplands heavy and golden with harvest, for orchards, gardens and beautiful woods in spring.

"You see," Isobel went on, "there's really nothing to keep me in England now. My father's dead, and I only have a stepmother and two little stepsisters. There's so much I'd like to learn here. I wish—will you help me?"

The word "learn" arrested Jean. It was plain in her eyes as she looked at Isobel. "But what could *you* be learning here?"

"A great deal," said Isobel, smiling at Jean. "About the way of life and the birds and flowers—"

"Mairi will be knowing about those," said Jean. "Yes, indeed, she will be telling you. But it is only in winter that there are wild geese and swans on the lochs and so many other birds. This month most of them are flying away, you see."

I looked at Jean, remembering that she also would be going away, and my heart began to ache again. I couldn't imagine home without Jean. Even Isobel's presence couldn't compensate for the parting.

I wonder now how Isobel felt that first day, alone among Gaelic-speaking people in a remote croft-house. Was she very sharply conscious of the bleak country outside, and the wailing west wind?

Yet I was to learn that she never seemed to need comfort and safe, warm things. Hers was an independent, solitary spirit. She never seemed to mind being alone. She would go off for hours on end, and gradually Mother grew used to her wanderings and ceased to worry about her.

At last it was my bedtime, but I didn't want to leave the group around the fire. "It is early and I am not sleepy!" I protested.

"Early! Indeed, no, it is late, Mairi, and you having to be up in time for school." Mother handed me a cup of milk.

"I want to hear more," I grumbled, and Isobel laughed.

"Tomorrow it'll be your turn to tell stories," she said.

I stared at her over the thick white cup. "But I will not

40

be telling the stories. It is the old woman who can do that. Oh, she is telling wonderful ones!"

"But you know them all, Mairi," said Jean. "I was hearing you telling Peggy MacKay about the Seal Folk and the Blue Men."

That was very different from telling Isobel, and I gulped my milk in embarrassed silence.

"Isobel has not the Gaelic," Jean went on. Her gaze rested on the old woman sitting hunched up in her chair. "But the old woman could be singing the songs for her. Some of them are very old. When she's dead no one will remember them, perhaps."

"Has no one ever collected them?" Isobel asked, looking interested.

"Mrs. Kennedy-Fraser—she who loves the songs of the Isles—was here once. She wrote down two of them, but there will be others." She spoke to the old woman, and the *cailleach* replied eagerly.

"The songs? Yes, indeed. But could the lass write them down? It must be very difficult."

Jean put the question in English, and Isobel nodded.

"Oh, yes, I think I could. I studied music for some years."

"Father Donald has a piano," I told her.

"Will you be going to bed now?" Mother handed me a jug of hot water from the great kettle, and I went reluctantly behind the partition. Of course I could still hear the conversation.

"Are there other songs?" Isobel asked. "Maybe on a little island like Glascreagh? If I could collect them, I might publish them later on."

"There was a great singer on Glascreagh, but she is dead," Mother explained. "Mairi heard her sing once years ago.

41

But there will be old Sorcha MacDonald. She will be knowing the 'Glascreagh Love Lilt' and the 'Milking Croon.' Maybe others besides."

I lay in bed, seeing the red glow of the fire over the partition. Presently someone went to the door and opened it, letting in a great draft. I heard Isobel say: "What a lot of lights there are in Alvadale! And yet it seemed dark when I was there. There's a steamer in. Will it leave on such a night?"

"I'm glad Martin and Neill aren't on the sea now," sighed Jean. "It was to take a week from Glasgow, then the long train journey. They may be in Alberta already."

"Far away across the sea they are!" wailed the old woman, since Jean had forgotten Isobel and spoken in the Gaelic. "And there was no need."

"There was need for them to go," Mother said harshly, in English. "The Western Isles are doomed! Soon more will go. It won't matter to the government in London if the islands are all given over to the ravens and the gulls."

Soon Isobel said good night quietly and came through the room where I lay.

"Good night!" I whispered, peering up at her black shadow.

"Aren't you asleep?" Isobel whispered back. She passed behind the second partition into her own corner. From there, so short a time ago, had come Neill's loud laughter and gay, assertive voice. Isobel lit a candle and I heard the splash of water.

I lay and listened and wondered, without any real conception of the change that had come into my life. For it was my life that was to be the most affected. Isobel brought interest and much joy to Mother and the old woman, and they both loved her dearly. But to me she brought color and laughter, new ideas, new speech . . . a whole new life. If Isobel had not picked me up out of that cold sea pool, I would, in all probability, be a different girl now.

But as I lay in my bed waiting for Jean on that stormy April night, I only thought that I would have a great deal to tell everyone in school when the morning came.

The next morning I awoke early and lay wondering if Isobel was really asleep only a yard or two away. I longed to look around the partition to make sure, but to do so I would have had to scramble over Jean. Her hair was spread out on the pillow; fine, thick hair, but not curly like mine. Her lashes, too, though dark and thick, were not as long as mine. No one had ever encouraged me to be vain, and there was only one small mirror in the house, but I had once heard Father Donald say, "Mairi will be beautiful one day. Will you be looking at the lashes on her and the sweet red mouth?"

I was not meant to hear, but I was glad that I had. Until then I had thought that I was plain.

I lay staring at Jean and the sleeping faces of Mother and the old woman in the other bed. The *cailleach* looked dead, she lay so still, and I began to be scared.

I could hear the cock crowing and the cackle of the hens. There was also the sound that was never absent any morning of my life . . . the long, harsh cries of the gulls.

Presently Mother awoke, and she rose almost at once, slipped on her clothes and went into the living room, tying on her apron as she went. I heard her raking over the smoldering peats and adding new ones, so that the fire would blaze up and the kettle boil quickly.

43

At the sound Jean opened her eyes and smiled at me. "You are the early one this morning, Mairi!" For usually I had to be very nearly pulled out of bed so as not to be late for school.

"Is the old woman dead?" I whispered, staring in awe at the gaunt yellow face on the pillow.

"Dead?" Jean jumped. "Of course not. What are you thinking of?"

"She looked dead," I answered, much relieved.

Jean got out of bed, looking very young and thin in her short nightgown.

"Hush!" she breathed. "Isobel may be liking to sleep late."

But we did not know Isobel. Jean had only just gone when bumping and splashing behind the partition told me that our guest was up. In a few minutes she appeared, bright-eyed and cheerful, wearing old, thick shoes and a very serviceable sweater and skirt. We looked at each other, I still in bed, with the blankets up to my chin.

"Jean was saying you might sleep late," I remarked.

"I never do," said Isobel, and all the time she lived with us she never once stayed in bed after we were up. I thought it silly of her, for there was I loving the warm blankets and forced to be in school by nine o'clock.

"Do you think I could milk the cow?" asked Isobel.

"She kicks . . . Oh, indeed, she will be kicking hard!"

Isobel went away, looking determined, and I was so eager to see what happened that I washed and dressed more quickly than usual.

I found Jean and Isobel in the byre. Isobel looked perfectly at home beside our difficult cow, and a stream of milk was flowing into the pail. Jean leaned against the stones of

44

the low doorway, giving our guest a Gaelic lesson.

Presently Isobel laughed and stood up with the pail in her hand.

"I just have to learn, but it does seem a difficult language. Fancy, verbs before breakfast!"

"Mother will be saying you must not work," said Jean, as we returned to the house, and that was just what she did say. She scolded Jean for letting the guest do the work of the house. But soon Isobel was learning to make porridge, wearing a big print apron.

I saw Mother smile a little as she bent over the fire, and knew that she was not really angry. After all, who could be angry because Isobel wouldn't sit idly on a high chair like a fine lady?

While Isobel stirred the porridge, she sang us an English song called "The Lark in the Morn." Her voice was very soft and clear, and it brought the old woman, half-dressed in her thick woolen underbodice and flannel petticoat, to the opening in the partition.

It was all very strange, I thought, as I fed the hens. Not in the least like any other morning.

Of course those first days were not always easy. Mother told us we must try to remember to speak English among ourselves when Isobel was there, for it was impolite to say things she couldn't understand. But we were always forgetting, Mother included. She had not spoken much English for a long time.

Isobel said we mustn't worry about her; she had, after all, come to hear the Gaelic. In a day or two she knew the names of quite a number of things, but the construction of sentences baffled her, and poor Jean felt she couldn't be a very good teacher.

"We must be finding someone else to teach you," she said. A thoughtful expression came over her face, and I knew she had an idea.

Isobel continued to insist that she wanted to help in the house, and she really seemed to enjoy it.

"And she paying twenty good shillings for just a bed and a share of our food!" Mother cried. "Terrible it is that she should also milk and bake and wash the dishes!"

There were other difficulties, too, for when five people are living together in a very small house, they have not much privacy. There certainly were crudities in our way of living, and maybe the worst of them was the nightly problem of getting the old woman to bed. She was very infirm and wore many clothes, and she was apt to be very irritable during the struggle. Also she could never manage to get out to our primitive earth closet. On our side of the loch only Father Donald's house had indoor sanitation.

At first we were scared that Isobel would be shocked and even disgusted, even though she couldn't understand the old woman's indelicate remarks, but we soon learned differently. When Jean had gone, she often helped, and then it was easier, for the old woman behaved much better.

I regretted the hours spent in school, for I was afraid of missing something. But, anyway, Isobel was usually only at home during the mornings and evenings. Every day she set off by herself, taking a walking stick and some food for a picnic. Those April days were sometimes sunny, sometimes wet and cold, but it made no difference.

"She is like a very small duck. Yes, indeed, and a very brave little duck!" Mother said one day, when Isobel had set off in a downpour, covered from head to foot in black oilskins. "Is that lass afraid of anything? You should have

46

been seeing her, Mairi. Jumping the boggy places and it raining so hard."

Sometimes Isobel persuaded Uilleam Angus to take her across the loch to Alvadale, and then she usually brought back candy for the old woman. She would have brought it for us, too, I know, but she was scared of what Mother would say.

One day, about a week after her arrival, she came back from Alvadale with a brown paper parcel for Jean.

"You mustn't mind," she said, smiling. "It's just a length of material to make a pretty dress."

Jean, who had never possessed anything that could be called "pretty," stared in awe at the soft material; it was finer and more gaily colored than any she had ever touched.

"But—oh, but you must not!"

Isobel held the bright folds under Jean's chin.

"I think I can make it up in time. I love sewing."

"But Mother will be so angry," whispered Jean. "She will say—"

But Mother said very little. I think she realized how much Isobel wanted to make the dress for Jean.

"Well, and is not the lassie deserving of a pretty dress?" the old woman cried. "You could not be refusing, Ceit."

During her last days at home Jean was very quiet, but her eyes burned with excitement and fear, and at night she tossed around in her sleep.

Isobel's first pound, which she had insisted on paying at once, bought Jean a pair of shoes and some gloves. She and Mother went over the loch especially to buy them, at the store on the pier. The next week a suitcase like Neill's was bought.

Those last days must have been a worrying, unhappy

47

time for Mother, far worse than I realized at the time. Her sons were far away in Canada, and it must have been terribly hard to face Jean's departure cheerfully. But she never once shed tears over the contents of the new suitcase.

Jean's fare worried us until a registered letter came from Glasgow containing money for the journey. Father Donald had offered to see Jean safely to Mrs. Robertson's, and, though Jean said very little, it must have comforted her to know that she would have company during the long night journey across the Minch.

If Isobel had not been making life so interesting, I would have felt much worse than I did. I was startled when Mother said to me, "We will be missing Isobel when she leaves us."

"Leaves us?" I stared at Mother unbelievingly. "But she is living with us now. Why should she leave us?"

Mother pressed her fingers into my shoulder and shook me slightly.

"She is not here forever, Mairi. Soon, perhaps, she will be tired of living on herrings and porridge. And she is not used to being in such a little house."

"Our house is bigger than the Beaths' or the MacKays'...."

"Yes, indeed. But this is not the life for her. She is very pretty; perhaps there is someone she intends to marry. She will go some time, *mo chridhe*. Remember that."

I did remember it for a day or two, and then Jean's departure was near and I forgot. For a while, anyway, Jean was the only person in the world who mattered, and I still prayed desperately that she wouldn't go away to Glasgow. But I knew that my prayers wouldn't be answered.

ROS MACBRIDE

On the day before Jean was to leave, Isobel, Jean and I walked over to the western seaboard. It was a Sunday, a most beautiful day, and Isobel had been with us for almost two weeks. The sky was brilliantly blue, and the sunlight was warm; the grass was springing up everywhere, the heather was green, too, and the *peat-hags* reflected the sky. In the crannies of the uneven stone walls and under the roofs of the croft-houses, glowed the round yellow faces of St. Bride's flower. A hundred scents came on the wind.

We walked quickly along the rutted, stony road, with Isobel between us. She always walked very fast, with her head up, using her stick. That day she was seeing the full beauty of the Isles for the first time.

Presently we reached the fertile *machair* that extended for miles along the western seaboard. There were many *clachans* on the *machair,* because the land was more fertile than in the east, and oats and potatoes were planted almost to the edge of the sea.

In front of us, beyond the white beach that lay below the *machair,* was the Atlantic Ocean, clear green near at hand and shading to indigo and blue where the St. Kilda Isles showed more than forty miles away. When we looked to the south, toward the Sound of Glascreagh, many other islands were blue. But nearest was the western side of Glascreagh; in the clear air we could see the waves breaking against the great cliffs and the gulls sitting in rows on the high ledges.

But I liked best to gaze westward across that great ocean, for Canada and the United States of America lay somewhere beyond, thousands of miles away. Also the remote St. Kilda Isles had always held a fascination for me. I had listened so often to tales of *Tir-nan-Og,* the Blessed Islands, that the idea of a mythical heaven on the far rim of the sea was in some ways more real to me than the New World.

"To think that by Tuesday I shall be in a city far away from all this!" Jean said suddenly. "Why, there will be no great wind there and no sea birds crying!"

"Traffic will make the noise instead," said Isobel.

Everyone we met greeted us and asked questions, for the news of Jean's departure had traveled far. They cast curious glances at Isobel, too, and we really had no need to explain that she was from England but that she was living with us now. We were invited into several croft-houses, and we had to drink many cups of tea before we returned to the shore.

Below the grass of the *machair* is fine white sand. The low cliffs are sand, held together by thick, coarse grass. I had never seen yellow sand, and took the lovely, silver-white miles for granted, but Isobel was lost in wonder.

To the north and south stretched the shore, bordered by the bright, orange-brown wrack, and we turned and walked southward, toward Polleray and Glascreagh.

"I haven't been to Glascreagh yet," Isobel remarked. "I'm waiting for Mairi to go with me. I want to try to collect those songs, and I'll need someone to write down the Gaelic words for me. But perhaps no one will sing for me."

"It would be quite easy if Ros MacBride were with you," said Jean. "We may be seeing him if we go this way."

"Who is Ros MacBride?"

"Oh, he is living in the *clachan* called Polleray and not on Glascreagh, but the people of Glascreagh will be doing anything for him. He will be living in quite a big house with his aunt, and he runs the Glascreagh mail boat—"

"And he will be very clever!" I added.

"Yes, indeed," Jean agreed eagerly. "He was born in the Isles, but he became a great scholar. He lived at Glasgow University and lectured to the students, but his health was not good, and so he came to live here and run the mail boat. It was very sad. As quite a young boy, only eighteen, he joined the army and was wounded in France in 1918. It was after that that he took his degree and did so very well. I was wanting very much for you to meet him, Isobel—"

"I'd like to meet him," said Isobel. "If he'd help me, I'd be very grateful. Because I have an idea. I didn't say this before because I thought you might laugh at me for daring to try. But if people would help me—Mairi and the old woman and perhaps Ros MacBride—I want to make a book about the Isles. Not really *write* a book, because there'd be everything in it; unpublished songs, if I can take them down and write accompaniments, and many of the stories. And there could be photographs. I've taken some already and I could take more. I know there are dozens of books about the Isles, but I'd try to make this different. What do you think?"

I was thrilled and excited by the wonderful idea, and so was Jean, even though she was going away. Hitherto books had been written by clever people in Glasgow or London, but now here was Isobel asking our help.

After a few moments Jean cried, "Isobel, could you make a book about the whole year? You were telling us about England on the night you came. About the fields being bare and the woods so green and the cherry blossoms in the orchards. And then you told us about the other seasons."

Isobel stopped and stared at Jean, and I said, "But here there will be no trees and no cherries and apples growing. *Nothing* like Isobel said."

Jean's face was flushed, and her eyes were bright.

"No, but we have other things," she said eagerly. "In the winter the land is brown, and it's cold and wild, and there are barnacle geese on the lochs. Then, in spring, the grass is green, and there are days like today. Then there will be the sowing and the peat-cutting, and after that the thatching and the kelp-burning, and the flowers that are here on the *machair* in June."

She paused, and Isobel said in a quick, excited voice:

"Go on!"

"In the summer it is never growing properly dark, and there are the Northern Lights in the sky; the Dancing Men, we call them. The evenings are quiet, and the smoke goes up straight, and the seals bay on the rocks at twilight. The oats grow tall, and the wind is in them here by the sea, and then carts will be coming home late, bringing the dried peats to be stacked. Then there is the autumn and the harvest. Not a great harvest, like yours in England, but we work hard and sing while we are working. Then the winter comes again, and the *cailleach* tells the stories while we knit and weave at the loom."

After that we walked on for some distance in silence. Isobel's face was alight and thoughtful, and even I had felt the poetry in Jean's long speech. In fact I had been astonished to hear my sister talk like that, giving us her picture of the Hebridean year.

"Jean, that's a wonderful idea," Isobel said gently at last. "That's how it shall be. Thank you very, very much."

"You made us see England," said Jean. "English people, and others, too, perhaps even in Canada, should be seeing the Western Isles."

"Yes, they shall!" cried Isobel. "We'll call the book *Hebridean Year*. The songs and stories all belong to different seasons, and they must all go in their right places. Mairi must help me. It'll be yours and Mairi's book as well as mine. When it's finished, you shall read it, Jean, and alter it if you like. It will belong to all of us."

As we walked on close to the water's edge, we planned how the book should look. It was to be a big one, so that the music could go in, and it was to have a sea-green cover with seven wild swans flying across it. Seven for luck, as the old woman always said.

After we had walked for about two miles over the hard sand, we saw the smoke from Ros MacBride's chimney rising in a spreading blue feather above the high rocks on the point. The western end of Glascreagh, more than a mile away across the mouth of the Sound, looked much nearer than that in the clear light.

"There's a boat coming from Glascreagh!" cried Isobel, pointing.

"Yes, it will be the mail boat," I said. "He will have been over to visit someone or perhaps to take the doctor across. He will have no mail to take until Tuesday, after the steamer has called." My voice faltered on the last words, for that was the steamer that would carry Jean away.

"Run!" Jean ordered quickly. "Then we'll be there in time to meet him."

She and I led the way to the point, and soon we were all far out on the rocks on the other side, where Ros always brought the boat in. There was no harbor at Polleray, but it was fairly sheltered there.

The Kittiwake was a large white boat, with a deep well in her for cargo and a tiny cabin that was usually crammed with buckets, nets, and sacking. She had an engine that was constantly failing, either from lack of gasoline or some more complicated reason, and it was quite usual to see her coming over from Glascreagh under sail. They were fine sails, red-brown in color, and I always liked to see them outspread in the wind. But that day they were rolled up, and the engine seemed to be running well.

Ros was occupied in steering her inshore, for at low tide the rocks were treacherous even to one who knew them well, so he did not at first notice our arrival. But after a minute or two he saw us and waved, and his broad face, red with the tang of the sea wind, lighted up. Like everyone else, Ros MacBride enjoyed having visitors. Very few strangers came as a rule to this desolate part of the coast, and we often thought he must get weary of his anxious, fussy little aunt. Some evenings, when he wasn't reading or studying, he was at Polleray Inn, seeking company.

I had liked Ros MacBride since he first came from Glasgow nearly two years before. In the first place I liked his appearance. Looking at him, you would never have thought that ill-health, caused by the old war wound, had driven him from the city. He had rather stiff sandy hair and very blue eyes, and he had a way of wrinkling up his whole face when he was amused. He had his moods . . . he could be very irritable, so people said. But he had always been friendly and kind to Jean and me.

I always thought of him as quite old, but I suppose he was only twenty-seven when he and Isobel met.

At last the boat scraped on the rocks, and Ros stepped ashore.

"Well, what a pleasant surprise!" he cried. Ros spoke "real English," though he was a Gaelic scholar. He almost never used the turns of phrase that marked most of us as Gaelic speakers. "How are you, Mairi? How are you, Jean? And is this your English guest? I heard that you had a visitor from England." He smiled at Isobel very warmly and took her hand.

"Yes, this will be Isobel Darroch," said Jean. "She has no Gaelic yet."

"Yet? Does that mean you intend to learn?" Ros asked. His voice still had the lilt of the Islesman, in spite of his "real English."

I never saw Isobel awkward or tongue-tied. She laughed and said, "Poor Jean! I've been worrying her to death. She feels she isn't a very good teacher. Yes, I do want to learn. That's partly why I'm living here."

"Jean is going away to Glasgow tomorrow night," I burst out. "Oh, Ros, Jean is going away!"

Suddenly Ros stood very still, and his gaze went to Jean's face. For a moment they stared at each other as if Isobel and I didn't exist.

"Is that true?" he asked softly.

"I am going into service," said Jean. "Father Donald is taking me to Glasgow."

"*Mo thruaigh!* How they go away from the Isles!" Ros said it almost to himself.

"I *must* go, Ros," Jean said steadily. "There is no work for me here, and Mairi will be helping Mother. And—and you went away yourself. First to finish your education, because the school here could teach you nothing after you were fourteen. Then into the army, and after that to Glasgow University. I shall be like you. I will not stay away forever!" Her face was very white, but her eyes were quite dry.

"Yes, you'll come back," Ros agreed. He seemed to have no doubts. After a moment he added, "What about coming out in the boat for a while? Would you like that, Miss Darroch? I've just been across to see James Campbell about two bulls he wants ferrying across tomorrow. They'll have to come one at a time, and it's always a problem. It's a grand day for the water, though the wind's cold away from the land."

"I'd love to go!" Isobel said eagerly.

"Can we have the sail up?" I asked.

"If you like, though the engine's working well today."

"Isobel would be liking the sail better."

Isobel laughed and agreed that she would.

Ros held out his hand, and she sprang aboard fearlessly. I saw his eyes gleam as Uilleam Angus's had done.

"Can you sail a boat, Miss Darroch?"

"Oh, please call me Isobel," she said. "No, I've never had

a chance to learn, because I come from an inland county. But I'd like to."

I sat on the gunwale, trailing my fingers in the cold green Atlantic. Isobel sat beside me, and Jean perched on the edge of the well, swinging her feet. The engine carried us away from the rocks, and in a hundred yards or so, the view opened out. We looked back the way we had come to the miles of white sand below the green *machair,* and we saw the long, high line of the hills north of Alvadale with the cloud shadows on them.

It was all sharply clear and of incredibly beautiful coloring; silver-white, soft blue, translucent green. And black . . . the black of the Glascreagh cliffs to the south, high and unscalable, with the sea at their base. A flock of gannets flew across the sun, casting their shadows on us for a moment.

Ros began to unfasten the sail, and Jean sprang up to help, but Ros said to Isobel, "I'll show you. Would you like to try?"

And there was Isobel, poised above the waves, struggling to obey his orders. Then the sail was up, the wind caught it at once, and the old boat skimmed over the shining water. Isobel took a red knitted cap out of her pocket and drew it over her untidy hair. Her hands looked rough and cold with handling the ropes.

"How long are you planning to stay here?" we heard Ros ask.

"I don't know. Maybe a long time. I'm very happy where I am."

"I could take you sailing, if you liked. You'd soon learn to manage a boat."

"Oh, Mairi!" whispered Jean. "He likes her! I am so very glad. Now he will teach her the Gaelic. You will see. I hoped it would happen like this. He has all those books, and he's so

57

"But we can teach her the Gaelic—"

"Yes, to speak it, perhaps. But she must learn to read and write it, too. That's what she wants. I knew he was the one to teach her, and I hoped so much we would see him today. Mother is saying he's the cleverest man in all the Long Island."

Maybe it was Isobel's simple, direct manner that made Ros accept her so readily. At any rate, she must have impressed that strange mixture of ferryman, scholar and recluse, for the next thing we heard him say was, "The Mullochs, who own Glascreagh, are returning to the mainland tomorrow, and their yacht is in the harbor over there. It's a beautiful boat, but in need of overhauling. You could come out in her any fine day if you're over at Polleray early in the morning."

"Oh, yes, I'd like that!" cried Isobel. "Thank you very much."

We sailed along the western shore of Glascreagh, where the cliffs gave place to level grassland and a stretch of silver sand. We could see the rough, primitive dwellings crouching against the low hillsides, the small gray church by the shore, and even two ponies with panniers on the one track the island boasted.

"Sorcha MacDonald will be living in that sheltered valley," said Jean, pointing, and Ros asked what we wanted with the old woman, who was crippled with rheumatism and bedridden most of the year.

Jean told him eagerly, begging his help.

"Oh, if you would be asking the old woman to sing for Isobel; she would do anything for you, Ros." It was not flattery; it was the truth. Next to their priest, the people of Glas-

58

creagh liked and admired Ros MacBride.

"Why yes, I'll ask her," agreed Ros, smiling at Jean's anxious face. "I'll take Isobel there, and if we catch her on a bad day, we must just go again later."

We returned to Polleray and crossed the sand and grassland to the solitary house, a quarter of a mile from the *clachan,* where Ros lived. It always seemed a very fine house to us, for it had a kitchen as well as a living room, and there were narrow, dark stairs that led up to the bedrooms. It was just like a house in Alvadale.

Ros's aunt, Morag MacBride, was waiting for us in the doorway. She was a little woman with smooth hair, and she always dressed very neatly in black. Her dresses usually had white collars, and she never wore the coarse woolen garments the crofters knitted and wove during the long winter evenings. I used to think she must be cold, living there on the windy coast and always so smooth and neat, with not even a shawl. She was Ros's only relative, for his parents were dead and he had no brothers and sisters.

She had a pink, worried face, and she wore rimless glasses on her flat little nose. Her mouth was always pinched in anxiety, and she fussed so much that I always felt uncomfortable. No wonder Ros was sometimes irritable!

The moment we appeared, she began to fuss around Ros, telling him he had done enough for one day without taking us out sailing in the cold sea wind. While she was still talking, she darted to fill the big iron kettle from a bucket and feverishly piled peats on the living-room fire.

"My aunt thinks I'm likely to die any minute," Ros murmured grimly, as he drew chairs close to the fire. "She'll fuss over the saints and angels in heaven, and maybe they'll be more grateful than I am."

59

We thawed our fingers before the fire, while Aunt Morag rattled and banged things in the kitchen. Ros filled his pipe, and, as he lit it, he asked for news of Martin and Neill, Mother and the old woman. I sat on the floor at Jean's feet.

Isobel asked permission to look at the books. I saw Ros glance at her once or twice as she wandered along the home-made shelves with an intent, absorbed look.

We talked so hard that presently I forgot all about Isobel. We talked about Glasgow and what life would be like for Jean, and Ros promised to call and see her if he were ever in the city. But presently Isobel sat down and spread some books on her lap.

"Irish Gaelic," she said. "Manx, Welsh, and . . . is this Cornish?"

"Yes, but you won't find many Cornish books," Ros answered. "There isn't much Cornish literature."

"But . . . then you're a Gaelic scholar? The girls didn't explain."

"Yes, I took my degree at Glasgow and then I lectured there until 1925."

"And you speak all these?"

"Irish Gaelic, yes. There's very little fundamental differ-ence between Irish and Scottish Gaelic. Manx also, and Welsh a little. I read them chiefly. You'll find a few Breton books as well; it belongs with Welsh and Cornish."

Aunt Morag brought in the tea on a large tin tray. There was thick bread and butter and a slab of plain cake. She fussed over the fire, rearranged the curtains, tripped over a stool and took away the lamp to be filled. Ros and Isobel didn't even seem to know she was in the room, they were talking so eagerly.

Jean poured out the tea, and I sat eating bread and butter, to which I was unaccustomed, and listening to the talk about

Celtic countries, though I didn't understand very much.

I think it was perhaps the first time I ever heard a real conversation. I had never before seen two people lost to the world, completely engrossed in an abstract subject. Ros sat with his great boots thrust out toward the fire, his hands dangling idly over the arms of his chair. He wore a fisherman's jersey and rough trousers, and the reek of his tobacco filled the room.

I don't know how Jean felt as the western sky grew wilder and darker and the Monach light flickered out halfway to St. Kilda. I expect the realization that, by the next night, she would be on her way to Glasgow swept over her at times in a wave of excitement and fear.

The glow of the fire died down, and Ros threw on fresh peats; the wind rose and tore around the house, and we could hear the roar of the Atlantic. But it was peaceful in that fire-lit room, and the memory of that time is one of my most precious recollections. Jean was there and I was safe.

But the spell was broken at last. They remembered the time, and Isobel cried, "We *must* go! Mairi, are you asleep? How bored you and Jean must have been."

"No," I said quickly. "I liked listening."

"So did I," Jean said quietly. "By tomorrow night—"

"You'll be all right, Jean," Ros said gently. "You're a brave lass, and you'll get on. But come back to the Isles." He went to a drawer and gave her a large slab of milk chocolate for the journey. Then he said abruptly to Isobel, "If you like, I'll come over to Glen Gaoth one evening and give you a Gaelic lesson."

Outside the wind was tearing along the shore, and the scene was desolate. I remember very little about our long, cold walk home, but I know I had much to think about. It had been a day I would never forget in any detail.

THE POOR
AND THE RICH

When Jean and I were in bed, I clung to her wordlessly.

"Go to sleep, Mairi," Jean whispered. "You are tired and so am I. There will be nothing to say . . . you know it all. I—well, I know you will be looking after Mother and the *cailleach*. And you'll have Isobel. You will be helping her with her book."

"Isobel is not you," I whispered.

But she would say no more. She kissed me and lay quiet. And I lay there thinking sadly how life could change. Only a short while before, I had been the youngest, the baby, and by tomorrow night I would be the only one at home. I knew that I would have to grow up and learn to be sensible and responsible, but it seemed too soon. And Jean . . . oh, Jean! How would she fare in Glasgow, away from us all?

The next day was dreadful. In school I couldn't concentrate on my lessons and got into trouble, and I quarreled with Peggy MacKay because she said that Jean would never come back to the island.

"My mother is saying girls hardly ever do," said Peggy. "They marry someone in Glasgow and are living there forever."

I *knew* that Jean would come back; I was sure of it, but fear drove me to a fury of temper worse than the *cailleach*'s when her candy tin was empty. I rushed at Peggy and pulled her hair, shouting angrily in the Gaelic. The teacher, Miss Shaw, separated us.

"Mairi! Mairi! You mustn't behave like that," she said. "I know your sister's going away, and it's very sad, but we must have sensible behavior in school."

Sensible! I'd quite forgotten my thoughts of the night before. I almost spat at her.

Isobel was out all day, so dinner was a miserable meal. I think the food nearly choked us all. And it grew worse when evening came. Mrs. Beath had promised to come in and sit with the old woman while we all went over to Alvadale with Jean, but, as the bright sunlight gave place to a bleak, colorless twilight, the *cailleach* grew more and more cross and unhappy. She wanted one of us to stay with her.

The moment Isobel promised to sit with her instead of going across the loch, she was quieter. For though she was hardly able to exchange a word with Isobel, she was very fond of her. Since Isobel's coming, she had been much more alive and interested in things.

I sat hunched on my stool and spoke to no one, and Mother

63

helped Jean to pack up food for the night. The two of them worked silently at the table until it was time to get ready.

Those last minutes were the worst I had ever known. The clock on the dresser ticked on and on, until I could have stamped on it or thrown it into the mud outside. Jean grew whiter and whiter, but proved her gallantry by the tilt of her head and the steadiness of her voice. Goodness knows how Isobel felt in the midst of our suffering. She was gentle and helpful, and she looked sad, too. She helped Mother to find her shawl and her strong shoes, and she carried out Jean's suitcase and laid the pack of food on it. At the last moment she whisked off the kettle and made scalding hot tea for us all.

Then the moment came that had been menacing us for weeks; it had been coming steadily nearer like the clouds that bring the hail and thunder in winter.

Jean ran to the old woman and put her arms around her, and the *cailleach* clutched her feebly, tears streaming down her yellow face. I had never in my life seen Great-grandmother Gilbride weep, and it made everything seem more dreadful. We all stood silently watching.

Jean did not cry. She said brokenly, "I'll come back. Yes, indeed, I'll come back. And I will be sending you the grand picture postcards and some chocolate with the very first money I earn."

"Everyone is going away!" cried the old woman. Then she drew herself upright and said more composedly, "Be a good lass, *mo chridhe*. And do not be coming back a stranger, like some of the girls."

"I'll come back just as I am," promised Jean. Then she drew away and groped blindly for her suitcase.

The old woman, blind also, dropped her stick into the fire,

swore in a way that made me jump, knocked over her candy tin, and shouted to Isobel in the Gaelic to find her a handkerchief. In some mysterious manner Isobel understood. Ruari was jumping around us, barking wildly.

We went out into the strange half-light. The west was still filled with the soft glow of early May nights, and the clouds were drifting away to show the stars.

Isobel kissed Jean hurriedly and turned back to the house. Her clear voice followed us as we walked down the track.

"I believe I'll still be here when you come back!"

I remember that my heavy heart felt lighter for a moment in relief. When I looked back, Isobel had gone indoors, and I could only dimly see the little house at the head of the glen. Jean didn't look back at all; maybe she couldn't bear to do it.

Down in the *clachan* many people gathered around Jean to wish her well. Father Donald was waiting for us outside Uilleam Angus's house and passing the time in talking to the old fisherman. Almost everyone followed us down to the rocks, and when the *St. Bride* slipped away and Uilleam Angus began to dip the oars, we could see the white flutter of handkerchiefs.

"Blessings go with you. . . ."

Maybe they did go with Jean. I think she had some kind of fundamental happiness, even then. She seemed to me the bravest, sweetest and certainly the most safe person in the world. And though Isobel meant laughter, new thoughts and ideas, nothing was ever quite the same again after that night.

There was great activity on the pier, for the steamer had come from islands farther to the north, and a flock of sheep was being unloaded. They surged around us, terrified and bewildered, a gray wave in the half-dark. Dogs barked, voices rang out, and at last they were driven onto the road beyond the pier. Then there were two young bulls to be taken on board, and there was more excitement. But I took no part in it, though I was on the pier at Alvadale long after my normal bedtime.

I was too miserable to care about anything, and I hardly even greeted Ros MacBride when he came up to us. He had come, he said, to see the young bulls safely aboard for John Campbell of Glascreagh, and also to wish Jean a safe journey.

We all climbed up the gangplank and found the stairs that led down to the steerage saloon. As we paused, there was a bustle nearby and a party passed us. The owners of Glascreagh were returning to the mainland after a spring holiday. Mr. Mulloch, a tall, dark-haired man with a commanding voice, led the way, and following him were his plump wife and a boy and girl. Everyone said that Mrs. Mulloch hated island life and was trying to persuade her husband to sell Glascreagh.

There they were with their rugs and books and furs! They went into comfortable cabins, and Jean, Ros MacBride and I followed Mother and Father Donald down the steep ladder into the thick atmosphere of the steerage saloon.

We all stood around forlornly while Father Donald went away to rent two rough gray blankets, which he spread on the hard seats. A few passengers were already huddled into corners, asleep.

The stuffy atmosphere and a strong smell of whisky made me feel sick, and a cold perspiration broke out all over me.

"Oh, Mairi!" whispered Jean, clutching my arm. "I am not able to believe that in the morning we'll be on the mainland, traveling in a train...."

Suddenly, unexpectedly, I wanted to go with her, without even the guarantee that I would be back in a day or two. I would have endured that dimly lighted place for the chance to go on deck in the dawn and see the mainland peaks . . . for the chance to step ashore in Mallaig.

There was great activity above—bumps and bangs and shouts—for it was almost time to leave. We went up on deck, and the cold air seemed ten times more pure than before. Eastward we could see the dark stretch of the widening loch and the dark curves of the headlands against the stars.

It tears at my heart even now to remember Jean's going. The shiny suitcase that wasn't leather, the toil that had gone toward the making of her few clothes. I can see her standing there in her short, shabby coat; it was threadbare in places and skimpy in the sleeves, so that her red, cold wrists showed.

A bell rang, and Ros MacBride took Jean's hand. She smiled up at him.

"I'll come back, Ros, indeed I will, in a year or two. But first I will be earning some money and learning everything I can in Glasgow."

"Don't learn the wrong things!" said Mother harshly. "And mind you are careful crossing the streets. Very dangerous the traffic will be."

Jean clung to Mother for so long, I thought I was to have no last word. But as Ros tried to draw me toward the gangplank, I ran to Jean and pulled at her arm.

"Be a good lass, Mairi," she said. "And don't let Mother get too tired at the harvesting. She was ever one for working too hard."

"Oh, you ought not to be going!" I cried.

"Help Isobel with her book," said Jean. "She said it should have our names on it, too. Think of that, Mairi."

But the thought did not comfort me then. It was killing me to let Jean go. What did I care for books with sea-green bindings and flights of wild swans?

Then we were back on the pier. The gangplank slid away, a bell rang again, and in a minute or two there was water between the ship and us.

So Jean went away, and the first part of my life ended. Change had crept into it with the departure of the boys and with the inclusion of Isobel in our daily experiences. Life changed still more when Jean went to Glasgow and, though it was often interesting and even wonderful, it was ever afterward uncertain. For I no longer had any belief in permanence, and there was always the fear that Isobel might go away.

That night on the pier, when Ros led me down to the waiting boat, I was so sick and so blind with tears, there was no comfort for me.

"She will get over it, yes, indeed," I heard Mother say to Ros, and her voice sounded harsh and weary. "Poor lass! Her brothers and now her sister. Oh, *mo thruaigh!* What is coming to us?"

"Slow destruction," said Ros MacBride. "But Jean will keep her word. She will come back."

"I am not knowing how long we will be here ourselves. . . ."

Huddled in the tossing boat, I caught the words, but they made little sense. *We* were not going away from the Isles. Then Mother said "Good-night!" and came clambering down the steps to take Uilleam Angus's hand and step into the boat. Ros called down to me, "Mairi, tell Isobel to bring you with her when she comes out sailing in the yacht. Come

68

Saturday, if it's fine."

I didn't answer—I *couldn't* answer—and his dark figure moved away.

Isobel was waiting for us when we reached home, and the old woman was in bed and asleep. She made fresh tea and saw that Mother drank it, and she told me to undress and get into her bed. She knew I couldn't sleep alone that night with Jean slipping away across the black waters of the Minch. And it was cold; already the stars were clouding over. It would rain later.

"I'm not *really* a baby any more," I whispered chokily. "Tomorrow I'll start being sensible and grown-up."

"You're not a baby at all," Isobel whispered back. "Jean's going is a sad and awful thing. But there will be things she'll enjoy."

"I know," I murmured. "And that's one of the things that makes me feel so bad." Already my English was growing more fluent. "If she is enjoying it too much, she won't want to come back, and yet I can't wish—I can't wish that she be miserable."

I didn't sleep much, and both Isobel and I were up early. I felt weak and sick and thought that my legs wouldn't carry me down to school, but Mother made me go. It was terrible to return at dinner-time and not see Jean at the door.

One day and then another went by. In school I was irritable and inattentive. I quarreled with Mary Campbell and got bad marks for my lessons. Miss Shaw was kind at first, but she couldn't let me go on giving silly answers to her questions.

Father Donald came back on Thursday, and he told us that the journey had been quite easy and that Mrs. Robertson was being very kind to Jean.

The men were busy all over the island cutting and stacking the peats. Everywhere one could see black gashes in the moorland where the fuel for winter fires had been dug out.

Down Glen Gaoth, near the croft-houses of Arbhar, the men of Glascreagh were busy, too. Each morning two large fishing-boats came over, and each evening, laden with peats, they slipped back over the shining Sound.

Alan Beath had promised to cut our peats, but first he was busy cutting his own. One afternoon when I came home from school, Mother met me in the doorway. She was actually laughing and pointing up the glen.

"That lass, Isobel. . . . Sometimes she is an angel from heaven and makes us tea when we need it, and sometimes she is the little brave duck walking in the rain. Now there she is learning to cut peats alongside Alan Beath, and he the quickest cutter in Glen Gaoth!"

Sure enough, there was Isobel toiling in the moist black earth beside the old crofter, and a pile of peats was growing at her side. She was wearing a pair of Neill's boots, very old and not much good, and her hair was tangled and damp with sweat around her pink face.

"Oh, Mairi!" she called, as I approached. "Shall I ever get the knack?"

"It will be hard work," I said, staring wide-eyed. A man quick with the spade could cut as many as a thousand peats a day. Isobel was always slow at it, but she helped us to make sure of our winter fires.

"You know, Mairi," she said at supper-time, "I love to think that we'll sit around *my* fires, the fires I dug out of the earth, and tell stories and sing."

"And write your book," I said, for the first time enchanted by such an ordinary happening as peat-cutting.

70

"Yes," she agreed. "It should be written in front of a peat-fire."

On the Saturday morning after Jean left, Isobel and I set off for Polleray. It was a chilly day, but blue and clear, with beautiful color everywhere, and for the first time since Jean's departure I felt a bit happy. Isobel laughed and sang and talked gaily, and at last I forgot that we had all three been together less than a week before.

We went over to Glascreagh in *The Kittiwake* with the mail and stores. When we entered the little harbor, there was a beautiful yacht called *The Flying Gull* moving at anchor.

"Is that the Mullochs' boat?" I asked, awed. "Are we really going out in her?" And Ros laughed and nodded as he steered toward the tiny stone jetty.

It was very sheltered there, and the sun was warm on our heads. Two or three men came running down to the jetty, and the stores and mail were carried up to the post office. It was a very peaceful domestic scene. Tethered cattle grazed placidly, women passed in and out of the little houses and children and dogs played on the rocks.

We went out to the yacht in her own dinghy that had been tied up by the jetty. One of the men from the island went with us to help Ros with the overhaul. The yacht had sails and a big engine and seemed to me a very splendid boat. I wandered in delight around the well-furnished cabin, testing the comfort of the bunks and looking into the closets. There was also a small kitchen, and Ros dumped a package on the table.

"Sausage and bacon for us all," he said, grinning. "They want it overhauled, don't they? We'll test the cooking arrangements."

"*The Flying Gull* is wonderful," I said. "But I am hating the Mullochs!"

"Why don't you like them?" asked Ros. "You've hardly seen them."

"I saw them on the steamer. They had cabins and were going to be so very comfortable, and there was Jean in that awful place right down in the depths of the ship. Mr. Mulloch has a loud voice, and his wife looks fat and stupid. I am thinking it wrong for some people to have so much and others to have nothing at all."

"A budding socialist!" said Ros dryly, and I stared at him, not understanding. "You're right, of course, Mairi, but it's the way of the world . . . especially this part of the world. It's no good being too bitter. Maybe, when you grow up, you can work for the Isles in some way . . . help to make things better."

"I will!" I cried, afire. "I shall learn and be clever. Will you be helping me, Ros?"

"Yes, I'll help you," he said.

I heard him mutter to Isobel, "This one shan't go to Glasgow to be in service."

As we moved out of the harbor, I went up on deck and stared at the islands, and my heart was filled with a feeling I had never known before. It was the beginning of real awareness, perhaps of ambition. Though I was only eleven years old, I began to see dimly that maybe one didn't just have to endure poverty and hardships. One could learn and fight and perhaps, if a miracle happened, help others.

THE GLASCREAGH
LOVE LILT

I enjoyed every moment of those hours on the Mullochs' yacht. First we sailed right around Glascreagh. Then we headed south and went in and out of the small islands that had always just been dim, blue rocks to me. Tanneray was inhabited and even more remote than Glascreagh, but most of the others gave homes only to sea birds.

We returned to Glascreagh in the late afternoon, and Ros took Isobel to see old Sorcha MacDonald. I trailed behind them, a trifle unwillingly, because old Sorcha was almost like a witch. She was twisted, ugly and bad-tempered. Last time I had seen her, her little yellow face, peering through the peat-reek that filled the tiny, primitive dwelling, had looked scarcely human.

The croft-house was built against a hillside, and it was so low, and the stones so uneven, that it might have grown out of the earth.

Her daughter met us in the doorway, smiling and eager, for Ros was always a welcome visitor. She was a woman of around sixty, gray-haired, tall and dressed in heavy old knitted garments. She was wearing a clean apron, not properly tied, so she must have seen us approaching and put it on quickly in honor of our visit.

"A fine day!" she greeted us, in the Gaelic. "But the wind is cold for May. Will you be coming in now? You would be wishing a cup of tea?"

Whether we wished it or not, I knew we would certainly have to drink several.

We entered, and Isobel began to choke and cough in the foul air, for there was no proper chimney, and the smoke had to escape as best it could through a small hole in the roof. There were smells, too, for it was such a tiny place and old Sorcha was never out of bed.

There she lay, with her yellow, twisted hands outside a dirty blanket. She had no English at all, and Ros talked to her in the Gaelic while Isobel and I drank our tea and blew our cold noses, for the stifling atmosphere after the sea air made us sniff.

Old Sorcha listened to what Ros had to say, and her eyes never left Isobel. You would have thought she had never in her life seen a stranger from England, and quite possibly she hadn't. Not many tourists found their way to Glascreagh, and certainly not to that little valley.

"She is wishing me to sing the old songs? But I am never singing now. I am old and very sick."

"She is wanting very much to hear the 'Glascreagh Love

74

Lilt' and the 'Milking Croon.' And you are not too old or sick to sing, Sorcha . . . remember she is a friend of mine. She will come back one day, and I know you'll sing for her then."

"The songs are forgotten," the old witch said sulkily. "Who will be wanting to hear them now?"

"Many people in countries far away. So she'll come again, Sorcha, and maybe bring you another present. The chocolates, Isobel!" he added in English.

Isobel smiled and bent over the old woman, handing her the beautiful box she had bought at the store on the pier. It was wrapped in brown paper, and the feeble hands tore at the wrappings. Her daughter helped her, and the old eyes gleamed at sight of the box.

"Perhaps I will be singing, if the lassie is coming again," she muttered, accepting the bribe.

"You ought to be singing without any presents," said her daughter, obviously shocked, though she must have known her mother.

"She is old and fretful," she said apologetically, as we said goodbye to old Sorcha and went thankfully out into the sunshine and pure air. "But it is not true that she doesn't sing. There she is crooning to herself all day long when she is not moaning with the pain."

Isobel was impatient to be told all that had been said. She hated not being able to understand the Gaelic, but she was learning slowly. She had understood, she said, a few words here and there.

Isobel sent to Glasgow for a fine blue manuscript book, and she also asked Father Donald if she could use his piano occasionally. It was the one luxury in his little house by the loch . . . or that's what Father Donald sometimes said. We thought he had several. It was a beautiful piano, and he often played it in the evenings when he wasn't busy.

Isobel went again to Glascreagh and sat in the hot little room for hours, listening to the songs and writing them down. Then she spent several evenings at Father Donald's house, working very hard. It was the first time we had seen her irritable, but she loved the strange, lilting airs and was not content with her attempts at accompaniments for a long time. Even at meals she sat with the blue book on her knee, jabbing with a pencil and sometimes humming to herself.

But in the end they were written down to her satisfaction: the "Glascreagh Love Lilt" and the "Glascreagh Milking Croon." One evening she took me down to Father Donald's house to hear them, and Father Donald himself sang the Gaelic words. I thought I had never heard anything so beautiful before and was astonished that Hebridean songs could sound like that. For always I had heard the songs (as of course they should really be sung) unaccompanied at a *ceilidh* or while people worked at the harvesting.

Isobel's eyes were shining.

"Oh, Mairi, I feel as if I've done something real and valuable," she said, as we walked home.

"I wish now that I had been helping you," I said. For I had not wanted to go back to old Sorcha's house, and Isobel had guessed and gone while I was in school. The school-teacher over on Glascreagh had left her class and had helped Isobel by writing down the Gaelic words.

That smoke-filled room and the tiny, bedridden old woman had a kind of horror for me. It wasn't only that Sorcha was witchlike . . . I hated the way she and her daughter lived. Their old "black house" was a primitive hovel, worse than most of the others. The Beaths' house, for instance, was clean and shining, and the smoke escaped much more efficiently.

"You can help me now," said Isobel. "You see, I can't sing the Gaelic words—"

"Oh, I can be teaching you that," I said confidently.

"I hope you will, but I want to make an English translation that will fit the music. You must tell me what the words mean."

As soon as we were indoors, I sat on my stool and took the book from Isobel. I stared at the words of the "Glascreagh Love Lilt."

"It is a woman waiting for her love, and she says her heart cries with the gulls and the sea is dark. But he is not coming, though she waits the whole night through. Then it is morning, and she still waits for her love on an island in a green sea."

Isobel's forehead was wrinkled in thought as she ate her supper on her stool by the fire.

"It's quiet you are," said Mother anxiously. "Indeed I will be glad when the songs are finished and we hear you speak again!"

Isobel smiled up at her. There was understanding between them now.

"It won't be long. In a few minutes I'll sing the Love Lilt to you in English."

She took a pencil and scribbled for a while. I craned over her shoulder to see what she had written.

> *By the green sea I wait for my love*
> *And he is long in coming;*
> *My heart cries with the gulls that sweep*
> *   the white shore.*

77

O my love! My love is long in coming!
But the night comes and the wind cries
    with the gulls
And my heart is dark and wild as the sea.

By the black sea I wait for my love
And he is not coming;
The seals bay by the rocks and the tangle-
    weed is dark on the shore.
O, mo chridhe! *My heart! The morning comes*
    and the smoke is in the air
And sad I am on an island in a green sea.

Later she wrote English words for the "Milking Croon," and the songs were finished. They were to be part of the book, of course, and every day Isobel added something new to it. She took photographs of the peat-cutters and of the boats coming over from Glascreagh. She took one of Mother and me at the door of the croft-house, with Ruari beside us, and this was added to two she had taken of Jean before she left. The pictures seemed a miracle to us, and it was very strange to see ourselves.

So, in spite of missing Jean, life was very interesting. A month went by quickly. Our field was turned and the sowing done before the end of it.

Jean's letters sounded happy enough. Mrs. Robertson was very kind, she told us, and the work was not too hard. She had ventured out into Glasgow several times, and it was a very exciting place, though the traffic had scared her terribly at first. She missed us, we knew that, and all the sights and sounds of home, but she didn't seem to be letting herself pine.

Three letters had come from Martin and only one from

Neill. They were settled down, it seemed, and enjoying life. In Martin's third letter, there were two exciting pieces of news. He had become engaged to a girl we knew slightly, who had emigrated with her family at the same time, and he was learning to drive the great trucks that were used for farm work. He seemed to find the second news item of rather more moment than the first.

"She is a nice girl," said Mother. "But I am thinking they will not be able to afford to marry for some time." She sat with wrinkled brows after reading the letter, and I wondered if she was thinking of the money the boys were supposed to be sending to us as soon as they could.

June is the most beautiful month of the year in the Isles. That year the days were warm, and the south wind blew over the budding bell heather in Glen Gaoth. There was a haze over the Minch, and the peaks of the island of Rhum were not often visible from the summit of Ulval. The sea was smooth and quiet, even when the tide was high.

Every day I awoke with a feeling of anticipation, and I no longer wanted to linger in bed. I would be up and helping with the work, and while we milked or fed the hens, Isobel taught me English songs. I still loved to hear about English people and the English countryside; and before Isobel had been with us many weeks, I knew a great deal about her childhood and schooldays, and about her stepmother and two little stepsisters. She sent home for photographs, and I loved to look at them.

She also wrote to her publisher and got me a copy of her book about Gloucestershire. I took it to school and showed it to everyone, and I soon knew it almost by heart.

Isobel had many books of her own, which had arrived in

a packing-case from England.

"Why do you have all those books?" I asked one day.

"Well, because there's something in each one that I love, or that makes me laugh or pleases me in some way."

"The old woman was saying the other day that you too often have your nose in a book," I told her.

Isobel looked at me thoughtfully.

"Mairi, don't you ever read? Aren't there books in school?"

"There are some," I said. "Shakespeare and Scott . . . but Scott is dull, I think. Most of the books are very old and dirty. Miss Shaw was saying she asked for more, but they didn't come. The little ones are having reading books."

Next day Isobel put *Treasure Island* into my hands, and then she was not the only one with her nose in a book. The old woman grumbled and asked what I was thinking of to sit with my hands idle, but Mother said very little. Anything Isobel did was beginning to be right.

Those June days seem really magic, looking back. There were such everyday things as milking and baking and learning my lessons, but they weren't important. The *machair* was in its full beauty of summer flowers. All day long the bees hummed there above the summer sea, and St. Kilda was lost in the blue haze.

Isobel was on the *machair* nearly every day, and she would return in the early evening, sun-flushed and radiant, with her hands full of clover and silverweed, knapweed and crimson orchis. After supper she would sit on the stone outside the door and make pencil drawings of the flowers; little trails of tormentil and silverweed that she said were to be at the beginning and end of each chapter.

She was very clever and could draw almost anything. She

made little sketches of houses and byres and a real picture of Arbhar, with the boats in the background.

For a while I was content to sit beside her and watch, but one evening I found a pencil and drew Ruari. The lines of his beautiful body came easily, and then I put in the curve of the glen to make it a picture like Isobel's.

"Why, that's very good, Mairi!" she cried, when she saw it. "It must go in the book."

So my drawing was put away carefully with all the other sketches, photographs and songs in a box under Isobel's bed. I felt wonderfully important because I had made a real contribution to *Hebridean Year*.

Some evenings we helped the old woman to the doorway, and there she sat in her chair, muffled in shawls and enjoying the sweet, flower-scented air. Sometimes people saw her and climbed the slope to speak to her. Then the *cailleach* was very gracious. She enjoyed holding court. I was thankful she was so different from old Sorcha. I was *proud* of my great-grandmother.

Ros visited us often, and sometimes Alan Beath came over and joined us. When we all gathered around the door, it was almost a real *ceilidh*. Alan and Ros sometimes had fierce discussions about conditions in the Isles, and I listened intently and strove to understand their different points of view. Alan took for granted the bitter, unrewarding toil and the gradual draining away of youth and enterprise.

"Sad it makes me," he said. "Didn't my only son go away to India and die there? But no doubt it is being God's will."

"God's will!" Ros exploded. "It seems to me God has little to do with it. I blame the government in London. They will let a whole area rot and not lift a finger."

As Ros talked, his hair literally stood on end, for he was

81

continually pushing his fingers through it. It wasn't only the Western Isles, he said, but the whole of the Highlands as well. The government should buy back the land from the owners—often, especially in the Isles, Englishmen—give the crofters grants and instruct them in applying modern farming methods. Once the mainland glens had provided a living, however meager, for thousands of families; now they were empty, and the descendants of those families were in Canada or New Zealand.

Isobel was silent, obviously straining to follow the rapid words, for, though the conversations began in English, they always became Gaelic long before it was time for Ros to tramp the long miles home.

Sometimes Ros brought books with him, and then he and Isobel bent over them and they worked so hard they hardly knew we were there. I could see that Ros liked Isobel.

"Why isn't Ros married?" I asked my mother one day. "Why does he live with Aunt Morag? He should find a wife."

"Hush, Mairi!" she said, frowning. "You will be too young to talk like that. I heard that once there was a girl in Glasgow, but she died. Ros has been having a very tragic life."

Sometimes I was too young and sometimes too old. But I knew about falling in love and marrying, whatever Mother said. And Ros was so nice I wanted him to be happy.

That was how it was, then. The long days, the undarkening summer nights . . . the singing of the men as they worked at the thatching, the bell heather turning purple everywhere. And a daily round of work that never seemed irksome because Isobel was there. There was more talk and laughter than there had ever been at home, even in the days

—and how far in the past they seemed—when the boys had been there. There were always things to be learned from Isobel and the books she gave me to read.

The old woman was hardly ever irritable because her candy tin was always full, and she had Isobel to look at and —as time went on and Isobel's Gaelic improved—to talk to. Mother seemed to find the burden lighter now that a little money was being saved. Martin and Neill had so far sent us nothing, but gone for the moment was the specter of a bad harvest.

Mother never talked much, even to Isobel, but Isobel called her Ceit and strove to do the hardest work. Mother, of course, wouldn't have that, not when Isobel was paying for her keep. Twenty good shillings and wanting to clean out the byre!

"It is too much she is doing already," she said.

And then, early in July, Isobel casually announced that she was going away.

TIME
OF SORROW

It turned out that she only meant she was going to the mainland for two or three weeks to stay with Uncle George, but that was bad enough. I wondered how I was going to exist for all that time without her companionship.

Mother pressed her fingers into my bony shoulder and said, "Mairi! Mairi! Was I not telling you she would not be staying here forever? This is no place for a young girl."

"But she's coming back," I said. "It's only for a holiday."

"This time she will be coming back. Some day she will really go away . . . remember that."

The *cailleach* was fretful and resentful.

"It's restless the young folk are!" she said gloomily, poking the hard earth with her stick.

Isobel must have known how we felt about her going. She must have known that that was why the old woman sulked and Mother was more silent than usual. But she said nothing to indicate that she knew we would miss her. She was fond of us, but two or three weeks would soon pass, and she was fond of Uncle George, too. It never occurred to me to think that she might be yearning to see other people and places. I was very selfish.

Uncle George had rented a cottage on the shores of Loch Lomond for the summer. It should not have surprised me, for I already knew a good deal about Uncle George. He wrote stories for women's magazines under a pen name, and he liked to stay in different places. One year it was Corwall, the next Yorkshire, and some time in the future it might be John O'Groats. He needed new backgrounds for his stories. I had even read one of his serials, though Isobel didn't seem to admire them much.

There was only one thing that comforted us. Isobel would see Jean, and when she returned she would give us all the news . . . tell us all the things Jean didn't mention in letters.

I begged to be allowed to go across the loch to see her off, but Mother wouldn't agree because the steamer sailed so late. Instead I went down to the rocks with her and stood there, waving, as Uilleam Angus's boat slipped across the calm water. Then I turned sadly and climbed the rough track.

When I reached home, the old woman was crying fretfully that she was tired and wished to go to bed.

"Now it is the bad time we shall have with her," said Mother. "And you and I are alone, Mairi. You must be helping me."

Between us we assisted the old woman from her chair into

the bedroom; then Mother helped her out of her clothes and unfastened her thick stockings. I stood by, feeling listless and miserable. The place felt stiflingly hot, and I felt as if I might be sick. I longed to climb to the summit of Ulval to watch the steamer leave, but Mother sent me to bed at once.

"It's pale you are, Mairi. You must go to sleep."

I lay in bed, feeling desolate and lonely. It was terrible with both Jean and Isobel away across the Minch.

The weather continued to be hot and windless. The islands on the horizon were hidden by a silvery haze that only lifted occasionally in the evenings. The bell heather was full out earlier than usual, and the waiting peats grew dryer and firmer every day.

It was hard to concentrate on our lessons when the summer sounds were luring us outside. Almost every afternoon after school, Peggy MacKay and I walked over to Arbhar and waded in the cool rock pools, or else climbed the hills where sometimes there was a breeze from the sea. We scrambled in and out of boats, and sometimes were taken for a short sail. We grew very tanned in the long sunlight, and we never had shoes on our feet.

Any other summer I would have been happy, but now I missed Isobel almost every hour of the day. The tang had gone out of life.

After Jean and the boys went away, we had learned to watch eagerly for the mail, and our thoughts were turned to places far away. Now I waited more eagerly than ever, and in a few days a letter arrived addressed to Miss Mairi Gilbride. Not to Mother or the old woman, but to me. It was a triumphant moment.

It was a long letter, written in English, of course, and I

had to translate all that Isobel said for the benefit of the old woman. She described the house beside Loch Lomond, where Uncle George was very happy, writing, cooking and swimming in the loch. She told us how she had telephoned Mrs. Robertson and begged a day off for Jean, and how the three of them—Uncle George had asked to be included—had had a picnic on the slopes of Ben Lomond.

"Jean is much fatter," she wrote, "and very much prettier, but otherwise she hasn't altered at all, so don't worry, Mairi."

Inside the letter were two photographs; one of the cottage and one of Jean. Much of the cold, pinched look seemed to have gone from Jean's face.

The old woman beat her stick impatiently on the floor and demanded to be told every detail again. Like me, she missed Isobel sorely and was forever talking about her. Every word from "the lass" about that world beyond the sea was important.

The very next day a terrible thing happened. I was toiling listlessly home from school when Mother came to the door and shouted. There was something in her voice that made my heart leap with fear, and, in spite of the heat, I quickened my pace to a jerky trot. Mother had disappeared indoors again.

When I reached the doorway and peered around the partition into the living room, I saw her bending over a little, sagging heap on the floor, perilously close to the smoldering peats.

"Run for Janet Beath!" Mother ordered, without looking up.

I gave another look at the awful scene. The old woman's stick was burning unheeded, the candy tin had scattered its contents over the clean sand, and the old woman herself. . . .

"Go quickly!" Mother gasped, and she took the old woman in her arms and moved her away from the hearth.

I turned and raced up the track to the Beaths' house. My heart was banging against my chest and my knees shook. Janet Beath saw me coming and met me in the doorway.

"Oh, please will you come?" I panted. "The old woman. . . . She looked dead on the floor by the fire! Her face was blue!"

When we reached the croft-house, Mother scarcely looked at me. She was rubbing the old woman's hands as she lay on the floor with a pillow under her lolling head.

"Mairi, tell Father Donald to come, and then ask Maggie Campbell to be lending you her bicycle. The doctor—"

"Is she d-dead?" I had to gulp hard before the last word came. The neat little room was lurching before my eyes.

"No, but her heart. . . . Run, Mairi!"

So I went out again into the sun, and the whole world looked strangely different because the roots of my life were again in danger. The weeks of hot weather had made the track hard and smooth. I met Peggy MacKay and had the sense to send her for Father Donald, then I went on to Maggie Campbell's. She stared at me anxiously when I gasped an explanation and asked to borrow the bicycle.

"You will not be riding for the doctor in this heat! Awful you look, child. John will go. But he is away down by the boats. Wait! I will be telling him."

"No! No!" I answered feverishly. I took the bicycle and rode through the *clachan*. I wasn't very accustomed to that mode of travel, and my sticky hands guided the machine unsteadily. At first my legs felt almost useless, but somehow my feet pushed the pedals, and I went rapidly to the doctor's house half a mile away.

I shall never forget that afternoon. I shall never forget the hot, sweet fragrance of the heather, and how brilliantly the inner arm of the loch threw back the sky.

Shaking, damp with sweat, my hair matted and tangled, I thumped on the door of the doctor's house. I must have looked strange and wild, and I couldn't speak a word at first.

Doctor Anderson had not long come from Glasgow, and he was quite young, with a pleasant brown face and hazel eyes. He drew me indoors, and his wife gave me a cup of tea. It was very hot and weak; not the kind we drank at home.

As soon as he was ready—only a few minutes—we rode back together, for the doctor cycled everywhere when he wasn't being carried in a fishing boat to one of the smaller islands. He was so calm and kind that a little of the horror faded. He asked a great many questions about the old woman and said that she might not die. Of course she was well over ninety . . . ninety-eight, he had heard, but no one seemed very sure.

"We are not knowing, either," I said. "Oh, she can't die when Jean and Isobel and the boys are all away!"

When we reached home, Mother and Janet Beath had got the old woman to bed, and Father Donald was there. I crouched on the stone outside the door, where Isobel had sat to draw her trails of silverweed and harebells and other flowers. I still felt scared and very lonely, and I found myself muttering a prayer that Isobel and Jean would come.

It was a long time before I heard the doctor's voice out in the living room. When I went in, there he was drinking tea. The old woman must be awake, for she was calling feebly. She was calling for Neill.

Father Donald came out from behind the partition, and

his face was very grave.

"But she isn't dead!" I cried. "I can hear her . . . she is still alive."

"Yes," said Mother gently, "but she is very old, Mairi, and her heart is weak. You would be very tired if you had lived for nearly a hundred years."

"Is she going to die?"

It was Dr. Anderson who answered.

"She's very ill. But I can't say for a few days."

"Oh, then—" I forced back my tears. "Then Jean must be coming home! She must!"

"No," said Mother harshly, but there were tears in her eyes. "Glasgow is a long way away, and Jean will not be leaving her work. The fare is too high, Mairi. We must be managing without Jean."

"Isobel has money. She would lend some to Jean."

"We would never be asking Isobel for money!" Mother cried, shocked. "She has given us too much already."

"Isobel would come if she knew!" I wailed, and desperate misery nearly choked me.

That night I slept in Isobel's bed and Mother had mine. I say slept, but really I was awake nearly all night long, hearing the old woman's weak, fretful voice calling for Neill. Around sunrise, when I could see, through Isobel's little window, the white mist lying thickly over the heather, the call changed to a plea for Jean. It was heartbreaking to lie there and listen, and I climbed cautiously out of bed and dressed. I plunged my hand into the wooden box where Isobel kept her books and drew out a volume at random. Then I crept through the room where Mother lay in exhausted sleep and the *cailleach* tossed and moaned.

I wrapped myself in Mother's heavy shawl and sat on the

stone outside. The mist eddied over the moorland and the loch, but it didn't reach where I sat. The early sun was warm, and I opened the book, feeling that anything was better than my hot bed and the hot air indoors. In an hour or two I would milk the cow, feed the hens and prepare breakfast.

The book I had picked at random was *Wuthering Heights*. I read the first few pages slowly; then something happened to me, and I was carried far away from the misty July morning in the Western Isles. Breathless and seeking, I read on. Oh, it was wild and strange and wonderful! I kept on, blind to everything but the story, until Mother stirred in the house, and it was time to start the day's work.

I took the book to school with me and read it feverishly during the eleven o'clock break. I read it at dinner-time and walked down to school still reading. Fortunately Janet Beath had come in to help Mother and there wasn't much to do.

Something in Emily Brontë's wild, impatient spirit found kinship in me. The reading of that book was a shattering experience. Maybe I didn't understand all of it, but I couldn't rest until I had read the last word.

Mother may have been relieved to find me so quiet. At any rate she didn't scold me for having my nose in a book. But something even more shattering than my discovery of *Wuthering Heights* occurred when I was going to bed. The old woman was sleeping quietly at last, and Mother's voice was scarcely above a whisper when she said:

"Mairi, Isobel will not be coming back if the old woman is to be bedridden—"

"Not—coming back?" Glen Gaoth was at once the only reality. I stared at Mother aghast.

"There will be no room, and it would not be right. A

young girl. . . ." But her voice was strained. There was no doubt that Isobel was very dear to her.

"She could be living with the Beaths, then," I said chokily, after a few moments. "But we are needing the money. We need Isobel, and we need the money, too."

"We will have to be managing somehow without it," said Mother.

So I cried myself to sleep, facing a bleak world. I wanted everything to be as it had been before, with the *cailleach* sitting by the hearth and Isobel moving around the house. There had been enough changes, and I didn't feel I could face any more. But I was careful not to let Mother hear my crying. For I was the only one at home, and in a few days' time I would be twelve. I knew that I had to help and that my childhood was definitely over.

It may have been the unusually hot weather, but many of the old folk died that summer. Only two days after the *cailleach* was taken ill, Mother heard that Jenny Campbell was dying. She lived all alone in a very primitive dwelling by the loch.

That day, in the early evening, when the old woman was sleeping, Mother said suddenly, "Mairi, I must be going to see Jenny Campbell. They were saying this morning that she will not last long. I will not be long away. Call Janet Beath if the old woman wakes and needs anything."

She smoothed her hair, though it was already neat, and walked slowly away down the path. I watched her, realizing suddenly that she looked very tired. Her shoulders drooped, and her feet dragged. She had been working in our potato patch when I returned from school, toiling in the hot sun.

The evening was heavy and eerie, and dark clouds were piling up in the west. The loch shone with a dull luster, and there were shadows on the distant hills. In the Isles there is not much thunder in summer, for it comes usually with the hail and storms of winter. But that night I knew a thunderstorm was coming.

It seemed strange and frightening to be there alone. Not so very many months before, Neill would have been sprawled in the heather, Martin would perhaps have been going down to the boats, and Jean would have been knitting in the doorway. Now they were all gone.

I wandered uneasily into the house. It was so quiet that I almost went on tiptoe. The clock ticked very loudly, the only sound in the silence. Ruari had followed me, and I was glad to have him there.

I peered around the partition and saw the old woman's gaunt, sleeping face. There was something about its smallness and ugliness that brought a pain to my heart. I thought how strange it must be to be old . . . to be near to understanding death. Perhaps, I mused, gazing at her, she would hear the unearthly music that came from *Tir-nan-Og,* the Blessed Islands, and perhaps a white barge would drift out of the radiant west one evening and carry her far away.

Then I pulled myself up sharply, rather shocked. That belonged to the stories; it was pagan lore. The old woman would go to heaven when she died and see the Blessed Saints. It seemed hard to believe that anyone so little and tired could be rejuvenated to that extent, but Father Donald said we must have faith.

The old woman began to toss and mutter; then she began to cry for the boys and Jean. Mother had forbidden me to write and tell Jean (or Isobel) about the old woman's illness, but I felt that this weary plea must reach Jean somehow.

I crept closer and sat carefully on the edge of the bed. For some time, I sat there listening. Once or twice I said, "It's Mairi. Don't you want Mairi?" No. The cries went on for Neill and Jean; only occasionally for Martin, and never for me. I felt sadder than ever. Didn't she love me, then?

The little room was very hot and smelled unpleasant, but I sat on, feeling that she couldn't be left alone to cry so pleadingly.

Gradually a change came. She muttered "Storm!" many times. At first I thought she had sensed the heavy, thundery atmosphere, but suddenly I knew it wasn't this storm, it was one far in the past.

"You should not go!" The thin, harsh voice rose. "No, you should not go! There will be a storm . . . a great storm. You can see it in the sky. Coll! Coll! Stay with me!"

My scalp prickled. It seemed as if the past was coming nearer, into the room.

"Coll! Coll! The boats should not go out tonight!" And then, "The lad should not go. No, indeed, not Ewen! Oh, *mo thruaigh!* The storm will break!" Over and over she cried, "The lad should not go!"

These shadowy men of whom I had scarcely heard were, I thought, my great-grandfather and my grandfather. Her stories were never of her own past, but I knew they must have been dead fifty years or more. They had both been drowned, and Ewen—who was my father's father—had left a very young wife and a month–old baby. All those years ago!

I couldn't run to call Janet Beath. Something held me there on the bed.

"I must go down to the shore. They are all down there. Where is my shawl? I shall be blown away! Was there ever such a wind? If the boats come in, they will be broken on the rocks." She must have imagined herself standing on the rocks by the wild sea, for she clutched the blanket to her throat with a bony hand. "The storm . . . the wind . . . the thatch will be off! Oh, *mo thruaigh!* Who will do the thatching when the men are gone?"

And then, "They are out there on the black sea! Oh, God! Oh, blessed, blessed Mary! Let the boats come in! Our Lady, Star of the Sea, help us. . . . Hail Mary, full of grace, the Lord is with thee. . . ."

But the boats never came in whole in that long-ago storm. They were washed up as driftwood as the days went by.

Suddenly the old woman sat up and looked full into my face.

"It's you, Mairi!" she said clearly. "It's glad I am that you are here." Then a spasm shook her, and she fell back, with a blueness on her face.

Ruari gave a whimpering cry and ran from the room, but I stayed there for a few moments. I knew she was dead, and I was no longer scared, only filled with sorrow. Yet there was comfort, too, because she had known me at the last.

Then I walked slowly to the door. Outside the scene was eerily lighted and quiet. . . . How quiet! Mother was coming slowly up the track.

ISOBEL AGAIN

At the sight of her my calm deserted me. I rushed toward her, pouring out floods of Gaelic. Since Isobel's coming we had gotten more into the habit of speaking English, but never in times of excitement or pain.

"The old woman is dead!" I cried. "I was with her, and she was knowing me at the very end. But before that she was talking and I had to listen. She was calling for Coll and Ewen. There was a storm. . . ."

Mother took me in her arms and held me for a moment.

"Are you sure, Mairi? Why didn't you call Janet Beath?"

"I could not be leaving her alone, Mother. She was needing someone . . . she was so little and so—so very troubled about the storm. But Father Donald should have been there. Oh, she should not have died without Father Donald!"

"Her soul is safe; Father Donald saw to that. He didn't need to be with her at the last." Mother began to lead me back up the track. "But I should not have left you all alone. I thought . . . she seemed quiet, and Jenny Campbell has no one. *Mo chridhe,* you mustn't be too upset. It is a sad thing, but better than if she had been bedridden for many months. You were a good, brave lass to stay with her."

"Jean should have been here!" I wailed, and Mother's gaunt, weary face tightened. Jean would have been a great comfort to us both, and the old woman had wanted her. But it was too late now.

"Go and ask Father Donald if he will come, Mairi. But you must not run. You will be sick." I expect my face was green . . . I felt awful. "And ask someone to take a message to Dr. Anderson."

Janet Beath had somehow realized that something was wrong, and she came toward us. I heard Mother speak to her; then they went into our house.

I walked down to the *clachan,* only then realizing that Mother had never doubted my word when I said that the old woman was dead.

There was thunder rumbling in the distance now, and the loch looked oily and black. It was so still that I could hear the sound of banging over in Alvadale, where a fine brick house was being built.

Father Donald gave me a book and left me in his living room, saying that I was to stay there until he came back. I sank exhausted into his best chair as the thunder began to roll overhead. The rain poured down, and in a very few minutes the hills, the houses and the loch had all disappeared. The window was open, and sweet, cool scents drifted in.

97

Soothed, I fell asleep, but in my sleep I could still hear that old voice crying, "Oh, blessed, blessed Mary, let the boats come in!"

When I went home through the refreshing downpour, I found that the old woman's body had been moved into Isobel's room. I went to bed almost at once and slept soundly in the cooling air.

In the morning I saw the old woman. She looked peaceful and small and hardly real, with the candles flaring around her. I wondered what she knew now . . . whether it had been the white barge or the Blessed Saints. I had a feeling she would prefer the Land of the Ever-Young, but Father Donald would no doubt say that that was wicked.

In a day or two, after a Requiem Mass in the little church down by the loch, she was carried to her grave in the churchyard. It was only a stone's throw from the water. Jenny Campbell soon followed her there.

Mother was not one for writing many letters, and it was I who wrote to Jean; a sad task. I wrote to Isobel, too, pouring out the whole story of that night in fluent words I had not known I possessed. I could tell Isobel every detail, except that we would not ask her for money for Jean's fare. But Jean was never to know how ceaselessly the old woman had called her name.

In a few days we had a sorrowing letter from Jean, filled with the need of home. And Isobel wrote both to mother and to me. She said my letter had been wonderful, and I could tell how sad she was that she would find the old woman gone on her return.

After the old woman's funeral, there was an orgy of washing, and almost every blanket in the house was spread on the heather to dry. Unfortunately the weather was no longer hot, but they dried in the end.

My birthday fell two days after the funeral. I was not in a birthday mood, and I expected little from it. Mother gave me a blue and white cotton dress she had made for me, and I was pleased with that, for I had so few clothes. There was no question of wearing mourning for the old woman, though Mother had worn a black shawl for the funeral.

The steamer had been in the night before, and I thought maybe there might be a present from Jean, but I never expected the honor of what happened during the morning. Uilleam Angus appeared in the classroom with a yellow envelope in his hand.

"There will be a telegram for Miss Mairi Gilbride," he said, so loudly that everyone heard.

I jumped up from my desk, absolutely astonished and a little scared. I tore open the envelope, and it was a message from Isobel.

"Many happy returns of the day, Mairi. I'll bring your present when I return. Love, Isobel."

How wonderful! It must have cost a lot of money. I read it aloud to the others. I was the only pupil in the school who had ever had a telegram.

"And I was bringing over two parcels for you," said Uilleam Angus. "They are at my house, so will you be fetching them before you go home to dinner?"

I certainly would! For the first time my sorrow lifted a little. And the parcels were very exciting. One was from Canada, from Martin and Neill; it contained a pair of soft leather slippers and a book about Canadian cities with a lot of pictures. Jean's present was a pair of red sandals. I had never owned any pretty shoes before.

Mother's grim face brightened as she examined the things.

"Everyone is being very good to you. You must be writing to Martin and Neill. To thank them, of course, but they are not yet knowing about the old woman."

I felt sad again, thinking how eagerly the old woman would have watched the unpacking of the parcels.

So the days passed, and gradually Mother and I grew more used to being alone. But I longed for Isobel's return. She had been away for two and a half weeks.

At last a letter came saying that she would be back on Thursday evening.

"She will be missing the old woman," said Mother, glancing at the empty chair by the hearth. The candy tin stood empty on the dresser and the stick, with the marks of burning on it, was leaning in the corner. "Sad it is that there are only the two of us left." She had said that several times.

"Will you be going to Canada when I'm grown up, Mother?" I asked suddenly.

Her face took on an expression I didn't understand.

"Who can say, Mairi? Sometimes I think I cannot be doing the work of the croft for many more years. Life is hard for a woman alone."

On Thursday evening Uilleam Angus took me over the loch to meet Isobel. It was gray and rather cold for July, but to me it was more magic than the most fragrant June twilight. Going to meet the steamer gave me a feeling of importance, but I could hardly believe that Isobel would really come.

I was almost dancing with impatience when at last I saw her blown fair hair. She was standing on the top deck, and I felt more important than ever, for it was only for the use of first-class passengers. I had forgotten my resentment over

Jean and the Mullochs.

It was a wonderful moment when Isobel came down the gangplank. She was wearing the new coat and skirt she had made from material woven on our loom. It was a soft bluish-gray, and it suited her very well. She wore a blue sweater with it and beautiful new shoes. Her cheeks were pink, and her eyes were wide and bright.

She put down her cases, took me in her arms and kissed me.

"Well, Mairi! Do you like meeting steamers better than seeing them sail away? How brown you are! It suits you to be so suntanned."

I was so shy all of a sudden that I couldn't speak, and she turned to Uilleam Angus and greeted him. He picked up the two suitcases and carried them to the boat, while we followed. Isobel still had her arm around me.

"Oh, it's good to be back!" she cried. "I had a good time with Uncle George, but it's wonderful to smell the sea again."

We were soon over the loch and climbing out on to the rocks. Then began the usual argument between Uilleam Angus and Isobel, for she always insisted on paying him half a crown each time she crossed the loch in his boat, and he.was always angry with her. Isobel always won, though, because she pointed out that if she were a tourist, he would charge her at least five shillings.

So Uilleam Angus pocketed the money and looked at her appreciatively over his pipe.

"It will be grand to have you back!"

Isobel actually blushed with pleasure, for it was a high compliment. The old fisherman had anything but a pretty tongue as a rule.

There were a great many people around to greet her, for of course everyone knew that I had gone to meet the steamer, and Isobel had made herself well-liked.

Uilleam Angus said he would bring up the suitcases soon, and at last Isobel and I were alone, walking up the track.

"You will miss the old woman," I ventured, and Isobel nodded.

"It will seem very strange not to see her there by the hearth. I was fond of her, you know, Mairi."

"There are only Mother and me now," I said sadly, as I saw her waiting in the doorway. Her gaunt figure was clad in shabby dark garments, and her face looked white and tired. Isobel's face was very tender as she greeted her.

"Oh, Ceit! You look tired . . . you've been working too hard."

Mother smiled at her.

"It's glad I am to have you back, Isobel. You are cold, and there is supper all ready and the kettle boiling."

Something happened to the living room as Isobel stepped into it. Her soft hair seemed brighter than the lamp. The whole place was alive again.

At supper we talked about the old woman, but I wasn't really sad any more, for Isobel was back, and she would be there every day.

It was very late when I went to bed, for after supper Isobel opened her suitcases and took out many parcels. Mother's face grew worried and proud, but the pride soon faded before Isobel's plea, "Oh, Ceit! Don't be angry with me. I love shopping, and I've no one else to buy things for. I saw this apron and thought it would be lovely for you when all the hard work's done."

The apron was of dark gray silky material with a white

pattern, and Mother fingered it wonderingly. There was a box of chocolates, a tin of little sugary cookies, and a large parcel of knitting wool; two lots, one rose pink and the other blue.

"It's time you knitted in pretty colors," said Isobel.

I was staring in awe and wonder, and I was amazed when Isobel thrust the last parcel into my hands.

"And this is your birthday present, Mairi."

The present was a box camera and several films, and Isobel explained that that wasn't all. She would pay to have the films developed and printed.

Nothing so wonderful had ever come my way before. The time of sorrow began to seem far in the past. I could take pictures like Isobel's . . . photographs of my friends, of Uilleam Angus by his boat, Father Donald outside the church, perhaps, and Mother in her new apron. I could send them to the boys and Jean and keep some for myself for always.

So I went to bed at last feeling blissfully happy. For what more could one ask? All the beautiful presents, and Isobel at home again.

School had finished before Isobel's return, so I was free to enjoy her company. Of course I had to help my mother, but Isobel usually helped, too, and then she and I went out together.

Every moment in her company was a pleasure to me, and on fine days we walked for miles. Isobel made a lot of notes for *Hebridean Year*. Sometimes we went to see Ros or other friends Isobel had made during her earlier wanderings.

On wet days Isobel sewed or put her notes in order, and I read. I had continued to dip indiscriminately into Isobel's books. She sometimes argued that I should let her choose suitable literature, but she never insisted. I think she realized that there was no holding me. I had discovered the magic of reading, and I thought that books could tell me everything I longed to know.

I was happy and well-occupied, and not even Mother complained, though I doubt if she had read a book since she was a girl at school.

GROWING TIME

Autumn seemed to come very quickly that year. August just sped past, and early in September school opened again. The sharp scent of bog myrtle was everywhere. The days were colder and often wet. The corn grew high and golden to the edge of the *machair,* and it was watched anxiously whenever there was a high wind.

As soon as I returned to school, Isobel announced that she was going to stay at Coronallt Lodge for a few days.

Coronallt, a great house in the north of the island, belonged to Lord Carlow, to whom we paid rent. But he and his wife were hardly ever there. For as long as I could remember, the house had been let every year to rich sportsmen from England, and we regarded them with suspicion and dislike, coupled with unwilling awe. For it seemed incredible that people could have so much money. They brought their cars and servants with them, and they walked the island roads as if they owned them, with alien kilts swinging against their white English knees.

There were many stories about the fabulous amounts of food and drink arriving in crates and boxes by steamer, and I always wished I could be present when one of them was opened.

This year Coronallt was rented as usual, and it was a tremendous shock when Isobel said casually, "I know the people at Coronallt. Their name is Mainwaring and they're a Gloucestershire family, friends of my stepmother."

"You *know* them?" I gasped, and Mother stared.

"My stepmother wrote me and told me they were coming. They've invited me to visit them for a few days."

"You're going to stay at Coronallt?" I faltered. I could see that Mother was speechless with astonishment. It seemed a long step from a croft-house in Glen Gaoth to Coronallt Lodge.

"Well, I suppose I'll have to go for a short time," said Isobel, glancing down at the letter that had come from the Mainwarings. "I'll be terribly bored, but they expect to see me. It's a very friendly note."

"She is a strange lass," said Mother, when Isobel had run outside to get some water. "She has money, and she is so very pretty, yet she is content to live the way we do."

When I had got over my first surprise, I was curious to know what it would be like at Coronallt, but Isobel laughed and shook her head.

"I really don't know, Mairi. I've never been to that kind of house party. The men will go off shooting or fishing every day, and the women will sit around telling each other that it's all too, too dreary."

"And fancy that anyone can bear to live in those poky little croft-houses! *Too* unsanitary!" I said, in imitation, and Isobel looked startled.

"Mairi, your English is almost too good now. But I suppose I must expect it when you've been with me for months. You don't like people who come to shoot, do you?"

"No one likes them very much. They have loud voices and are sometimes rude. But they don't come much this side of the loch."

In a day or two Isobel departed with Uilleam Angus, taking with her almost all the clothes she possessed. A car met her on the pier, and for nearly a week she disappeared beyond our ken. She had actually suggested that, if I was so curious about the ways of English people, she would ask them to invite me to tea.

"They'd send a car down to Alvadale for you," she said. "Nothing could be simpler."

But I shrank from the idea in surprise and fear. Mairi Gilbride go to Coronallt to tea! I was still very shy, though not with Isobel. Mother shook her head, and the old proud look was on her face, so Isobel didn't press the matter.

When she returned, she had many stories to tell. She made us laugh, for it seemed a very silly way of living.

Isobel's visit to Coronallt caused a sensation among our neighbors, though she certainly didn't broadcast the news of her invitation. But when she came back, she was just the same as ever, and people soon forgot about it.

After the middle of September the weather became suddenly intensely brilliant. The sun shone all day long, and the air was warm again. The oats ripened, and Isobel gave up working on her collection of stories and legends for the book to toil all day beside Mother in our own small patch. When I returned from school, I worked with them, and at the same time we talked and sang. Isobel never seemed to mind how hard she worked. Often Mother tried to make her rest, but she only laughed and kept on.

When our own oats were cut and standing in shocks to dry, Isobel often went over to the *machair* and helped there. All over the island—all over the Isles, in fact—everyone was working feverishly, taking advantage of the good weather. For who knew how soon the gales might come? In other years the oats had sometimes been uncut in October.

Isobel said it made her drunk with color to work on the golden *machair,* close to the white shore and the intensely green ocean. I went with her once or twice on Saturdays and, through her eyes, the island seemed more beautiful than ever before. Inland one looked over the high, waving gold to the flat green country strewn with tiny, shiny *lochans.* In the northeast, three or four miles away, the long, undulating line of hills stood out sharply in the clear air.

The workers on the *machair* soon took Isobel's presence for granted, especially as, by that time, she understood the Gaelic fairly well. She worked bareheaded, wearing her oldest clothes.

Harvesting is very difficult in the Isles, for often the sheaves of oats have to be carted a mile or two to the stackyards, and not every crofter has a cart. But that year the harvest was in well before the autumn gales swept the Long Island.

At home we settled down contentedly enough to the long, bleak winter months. At last Isobel found time to work steadily at her book, and of course I had to help by repeating the old woman's stories. She had collected others from different sources, and one or two more songs. Her typewriter arrived from England, and it seemed like magic when the pages came out of the machine as good as printed. I liked to watch Isobel's flying fingers. Later she taught me how to use it, and I often wrote letters on it to the boys and Jean. In return Mother taught Isobel to weave on our loom, but for a long time she was very slow and awkward.

All summer Ros MacBride had been a constant visitor, and he came more frequently still on the long, dark evenings. We grew to expect his thundering double knock and his appearance in the lamplight, red-cheeked and bright-eyed, with the rain dripping off his oilskins. He always asked immediately about Jean and read her latest letter. He told us that Jean occasionally wrote to him, but it was good to have extra news.

Then he and Isobel would sit down at the table together and the Gaelic lesson would start. I often joined in, and I began to learn something about Gaelic literature and poetry. I found the lessons deeply satisfying, and ordinary school lessons after that seemed dull and uninspired. After all, Ros was reputed to be the greatest scholar in the Long Island, and poor Miss Shaw could hardly compete with him.

I worked very hard in school, though, and I began to take it for granted that I would have high marks . . . higher than almost anyone, though there were boys and girls of nearly fourteen, and I was only twelve. My only close rival was a boy called Malcolm MacNeil, but we were very good friends. Malcolm would soon be fourteen, the age at which everyone left the school. He was one of the lucky ones. He was going to live with an aunt in Glasgow and continue his education, and his mother said proudly that she was sure he would win a bursary to college. She was a widow like my mother and worked a croft alone, but she was very ambitious for Malcolm.

The winter evenings did not always pass in peaceful study, for Isobel's eager, questing mind would not accept opinions and facts without comment and sometimes criticism. I began to realize how much both she and Ros enjoyed an argument, and I would listen for hours, occasionally venturing an opinion myself.

Once, when I saw Ros looking at Isobel's flushed face and tumbled hair, I thought in a sudden flash, I wish he'd marry her. I wish they'd fall in love, and then Isobel would never go away from the island.

It would mean, of course, that she wouldn't live with us, but it would be something to know that she would be only a few miles away forever. Isobel would want to marry someone, so it would be a fine solution if it were Ros.

I told my thoughts to Mother in private, and she smiled and sighed and shook her head.

"I have been thinking that, too, Mairi. It may be that it will work out that way. Ros enjoys her company . . . Oh, yes, indeed, anyone can see that. But I am having a strange feeling that he will marry someone else."

"But who could he marry?" I asked, puzzled. "He seems to meet no other girls. Of course there's Sheila MacBlane at Polleray. She is very pretty, but she has no brains. And the schoolteacher over on Glascreagh."

But Mother wouldn't comment anymore.

Isobel had made friends with the doctor's wife and had an invitation to visit them whenever she pleased, but she wasn't out many evenings. Mrs. Anderson had friends in

Barra, and, on hearing about Isobel's book, they sent her an invitation to visit them during the winter and see if she could find any unpublished Barra lore.

But October and November passed, and she had not gone. I wondered if it was because of Ros's visits, but it was just as likely to be the wildness of the Minch. It was a long way to Castlebay and, though Isobel was a good sailor, it was likely to be an unpleasant trip in that wild weather. Sometimes the steamers were hours late, and when they did reach the comparative calm of Loch Alvadale, a few yellow-faced, wretched passengers came ashore.

Others beside Ros MacBride came to our house some evenings—Uilleam Angus, the Beaths and Father Donald—and then it was a real *ceilidh* . . . even more than when we gathered around the door in summer. We sang and talked and told the old tales until very late.

I was never sent to bed on those evenings, but sometimes, when it grew late, the faces wavered a little in the haze of peat-smoke and tobacco. It was when we sang the old songs that all my longing for Jean came back, and it seemed cruel and wrong that she was not at home. But she wrote that she was happy enough; she was attending lectures on her evening off. Yet there was still yearning for home in her letters.

I didn't think of Martin and Neill quite so much. It seemed years since they had gone away. Martin was married, and he had given up farming after only a few months. He and his wife had moved to Winnipeg, where Margaret had an aunt. Martin was working in a garage, for he had discovered that he was wonderful with engines. Neill had already sent a little money home, but Martin hadn't sent a penny. I supposed it was because being married was so expensive.

The storms seemed to go on forever that winter, and the thatch was loosened on a number of houses. At first I think Isobel was frightened by the fury of the wind, especially at night when we lay in bed, almost rocked by the gales.

All day long the air was filled with the cries of sea birds. In winter there were wild swans and lag and barnacle geese on the numerous *lochans,* and every type of gull. Isobel soon learned to identify them all, and I thought one of the best chapters in her book was a description of a winter afternoon.

At the end of January she made up her mind and went to Barra for a week or two. I felt sad at the thought of losing her again, but knew better than to say so. Isobel was fond of us, but I realized by then that we couldn't try to hold her.

All winter Ros had lent us both books, and sometimes we used to go down to Polleray on weekends to read or work in his comfortable living room. While Isobel was away, I went alone to browse along the shelves. He had all kinds of books, not just Celtic ones, and it was wonderful to have such a choice. Aunt Morag was very nice to me and fed me with ham sandwiches and fruit cake, but I was always glad when she had stopped fussing around the room. Ros wasn't always there, but he was very kind when he came in. He talked to me almost as if I were grown-up.

When Isobel came back from Barra, she began to teach me French, for she knew the language well. I thought at first Mother might say it was a waste of time, but all she said was, "I suppose it will be doing no harm. Learning is a fine thing to have."

It may seem that I was always with Isobel or Ros, but this wasn't really so. I was often with Peggy MacKay or Malcolm MacNeil, and we had plenty of fun together. But in a way

I enjoyed the adult company best.

Surprisingly soon the flower of St. Bride showed in sheltered places, and it was nearly a year since the emigration; nearly a year since I had met Isobel and taken her home.

When May came, it was a month of great beauty. Late snow fell thickly more than once, covering everything with a dazzlingly white sheen. The sky was intensely blue, and the sun shone. From the summit of Ulval I could see far across the Minch. The peaks of Rhum seemed near, and the Cuillin of Skye gleamed like the turrets of a fairy castle, unbearably beautiful. Isobel took photographs frantically and added the best to her book, which was by then ready to be sent to London. There was never much doubt about its fate. The publishers of her other book had received the idea with enthusiasm, and soon after they received the manuscript, they wrote to say it would be published in the autumn.

I knew I had grown mentally during that year, and I must have altered physically, too. For Isobel took a photograph of me and sent it to Jean, and in her next letter Jean said she would hardly have known me.

It was at the end of June that the miracle happened. One day Isobel came in with a letter from Uncle George and told us that he had taken a cottage in Glen Nevis, near Fort William. My heart sank, for of course it would mean that Iosbel would go away again. I could hardly believe my ears when she said, "Mairi, would you like to go with me? Uncle George says there's plenty of room, and it's time you went to the mainland."

I stared at her, breathless and incredulous.

"Me? Go on the steamer with you and travel in a train?"

When she nodded, I disgraced myself utterly. I burst into tears and ran to the summit of Ulval.

ACROSS
THE MINCH

As soon as I reached the top of Ulval, I felt ashamed. It had been a stupid, babyish way to behave, and I had been feeling so grown-up. I would soon be thirteen, and yet there I was crying and rushing away when Isobel made her wonderful suggestion.

I had done it because the whole idea seemed so unbelievable. Such an impossible dream.

"And of course," I told myself, as I scrubbed my eyes quite dry and started slowly down the hill again, "Mother won't let me go. She'll be saying the fare costs too much."

I knew Mother had managed to save some money during the past year, but it was for emergencies and not so that I could go adventuring with Isobel to the mainland.

By the time I approached our house, I was sadly convinced that I would be staying right there while Isobel sailed away to Mallaig. I entered the living room and began a shameful apology.

"I'm sorry," I mumbled. "I. . . . You see, I'd like to go so much. I can't imagine. . . . I knew it couldn't be true. You would never let me go, Mother."

"You are going," Mother retorted, rather harshly.

She was sitting at the loom, and Isobel was peeling potatoes, looking quite calm.

"Going?"

"Yes, indeed. At first I was saying the fare was too much, and Isobel would not want to be bothered with you, when she has you every day. And then you have no good clothes. But Isobel is saying—"

"Of course I want you, Mairi," Isobel said gently. "Think what fun I shall have showing you everything. It's time you left the island . . . you can't stay here forever."

"Many people do," I whispered, still not able to believe in the reality.

"Well, you shan't. Here you are, almost thirteen, and never seen a tree or a train. You've earned the trip by helping so much with the book. The fare isn't so much for a child, and Uncle George wouldn't care if half a dozen girls arrived at his cottage. As for clothes . . . the older they are the better. Who wants new clothes in the wilds of Glen Nevis?"

"When. . . . Oh, when will we go?" I gasped.

"In about three days' time. I shall send a telegram to Uncle George."

I knew where Fort William was; one of the things Isobel had taught me was to enjoy maps. It wasn't very near Glasgow, but the railway line went on there.

"Could we see Jean?"

"Yes, we'll have to try. Maybe she can come part of the way to meet us. Crianlarich or somewhere like that. We'll telephone Mrs. Robertson when we get there and fix it."

I was nearly frantic with excitement, but I didn't dare show my wild exultation to Mother. She might say it was bad for me and change her mind.

There was one thing. The visit to the mainland would take me away from school for more than two weeks, for lessons didn't finish until the end of the third week in July. But Isobel and Miss Shaw knew each other and sometimes went walking together, and Isobel arranged it somehow. Maybe she argued that a visit to the mainland would be more of an education than two weeks of ordinary schooling.

Had it been necessary to wait more than three days, I should probably have been ill. I couldn't sleep; all night long thoughts raced through my mind in an endless, colored stream. I lived in hourly fear that a telegram would come from Uncle George saying he couldn't have us after all. I expected to start measles or mumps, or else I imagined Isobel with a sprained ankle or some other suffering that would make it impossible to travel.

At school I felt very important. Only Malcolm had ever been to the mainland. One girl had been to the island of Canna once to stay with an aunt, but that wasn't like going to Fort William.

One thing worried me. I hated leaving Mother alone. But that problem was easily settled, for Alan Beath was going over to St. Kilda with some of the other men, and Janet agreed that she and Mother might as well keep each other company.

The weather had not been as hot as usual, but the day we

were to leave was warm and radiant. I hardly know how I lived through the hours, for the steamer always sailed late in the evening. My shabby suitcase was packed, and Isobel said I was to wear a warm jersey and a coat for the night journey. She knew I wouldn't sleep, so we planned to spend the night on deck if it stayed fine.

She also said she had ordered a flask of coffee and a packed supper from the Alvadale Hotel.

"I know you won't eat, Mairi, until we're away," she said, smiling. "You needn't worry about her, Ceit. I'll look after her."

Mother nodded and said she had no doubt of that.

When at last we crossed the loch in Uilleam Angus's boat, I was ice cold and shivering, in spite of my warm skirt and jersey and the thick scarf tucked into my coat. All feeling seemed to have left me, except for a dreamy incredulity. It *could* not be Mairi Gilbride who sat there, with her suitcase labeled: "Achonree Cottage, Glen Nevis, Invernesshire." I had seen so many people sail away, and now I was going away myself.

"Do stop shivering, Mairi!" Isobel said, laughing a little. "It isn't cold at all. Oh, well, you'll be all right once we sail."

I was better, however, as we pushed our way through the crowd on the quay, for a warm summer night brought out many people, and I saw a number of familiar faces.

It was very late, but of course it wasn't dark. I know no words that adequately describe the luminous quality of the sky. My legs shook as I climbed the gangplank, but I no longer felt sick and cold. I stood on deck while Isobel went to collect our supper from the hotel and to rent chairs and blankets from a steward.

I shall never forget that night . . . the moment when the

gangplanks were removed and the steamer slipped away from the pier. I gripped the cold rail and stared at the lights and the blurred faces, at the wide, shining curves of the loch and Uilleam Angus's boat creeping back to our own shore. I felt a moment of homesickness so acute that I thought, If I'd been Jean, going away for so long, I should have died!

But I *was* coming back, and my thoughts soon turned to the wider world beyond the Minch.

Hour after hour we sat on deck under the glowing sky, our eyes on the glimmering, waveless sea. Once or twice I dozed, but I never really slept. We did not talk much. Isobel read some of the time; it was quite light enough for that.

In the middle of the night we passed Rhum; beautiful, sleeping island. I had known the tapering peaks all my life. I said, "Oh, Isobel!" and threw off the rugs and ran to the rail.

Isobel followed me and said, "No wonder people talk about the 'Magic West.' On a night like this one forgets all the problems. Every one of the old woman's stories could be true."

Hesitantly, as we passed quite near to Skye, and I looked at the ghostly peaks, I tried to express my gratitude.

"To bring me . . . I never expected. . . . Oh, Isobel, thank you!"

And she laughed a little and patted my hand.

"It was time, Mairi. You've learned all your island can teach you."

"But I'll go back. It's my home, isn't it? I may live there all my life."

"You may, but I doubt it. You have to see another world."

As we drew in toward the strange, flat shape of the island of Eigg we saw the ferryboat coming toward us, carrying three passengers. The sky's radiance, which had darkened during the last hour or two, was giving place to daylight. We could see the great mainland hills; the mountains of Knoydart, touched with cloud.

Isobel led me into the almost-deserted first-class dining room and ordered coffee and toast. With a pang of sorrow, I remembered Jean, and how she had spent the whole night in the steerage saloon. It seemed wrong that I should travel in such peace and luxury under a summer sky.

I had never tasted coffee until that night and I found it a strange, interesting drink. But I gulped it as quickly as I could and reluctantly ate two pieces of toast. I intended to be up on deck again well before we reached Mallaig.

The sun was up as we drew in to the long, stone quay, and I saw the roofs of what seemed to me a big town. There were yachts at anchor in the dark green water, their white paint showing up against the rocky shores. To the north was the Sound of Sleat, with Skye on the one side and the mainland mountains on the other. Over the whole scene hundreds of gulls screamed loudly.

I stared so hard that my eyes ached. As I followed Isobel down the gangplank I remembered a sentence from Jean's first letter, "At Mallaig there were great high railway trucks, and a smell of kippers from the factory on the quay, which made me feel seasick again."

There certainly was a pungent aroma in the air, and the freight trucks were so enormous that I felt they would slide off the rails and crush me. But I never thought of feeling sick. I felt wonderful.

"Where are the trains?" I asked, picking my way around barrels and crates. "The real trains that go to Fort William?"

"The station's just along there," said Isobel. "But we're not going to Fort William until we've had a proper breakfast, Mairi."

It was not very much after six o'clock as we walked through what Isobel said was only a little town. Isobel chose a hotel where a girl was already polishing brass on the door and asked how soon we could have breakfast. The girl disappeared and soon returned to say we could have it at seven o'clock. So we left our suitcases and walked around, while I exclaimed over everything.

All my life my main diet had consisted of potatoes, herrings, porridge and oatcakes, so even the imminent train journey lost some of its importance when I was faced with that wonderful breakfast. There was grapefruit, a piece of deliciously browned plaice, bacon and eggs, toast and marmalade, and then—just in case we should still be hungry—creamy scones and raspberry jam.

"Will it be like this all the time?" I asked. Isobel nodded.

"Something like this. I've told you that Uncle George is a good cook."

"It seems strange that a man should cook."

"Some of the best cooks in the world are men. Uncle George says he just had to learn, because he lives alone and he couldn't bear to have a housekeeper."

I was nearly bursting with curiosity and too much breakfast as I followed Isobel into the railroad station. And there was the train, long and shining. It had "Mallaig, Fort William, Glasgow and King's Cross" written all along it, but I didn't know then that King's Cross meant London.

Isobel found an empty compartment, and we put our suitcases in the rack. I leaned out the window when the whistle blew. We were off! I was in a train. At first I wasn't sure that I liked the swift motion. But soon I was so enthralled I forgot to be scared.

Imagine seeing larchwoods for the first time on a summer morning in the Highlands. Imagine seeing fir trees marching up the lower slopes of the hills and the brilliant green of oak and ash. Imagine seeing the great bare hills of Sunart when you had all your life lived among little hills and mile on mile of *peat-hags* and *lochans*. I hardly spoke, but I leaped from one side to the other, seeing new wonders with every mile.

Trees, the blue stretch of Loch Morar and thin white torrents looping the mountain slopes. On the little station platforms there were flowers, and through the open windows came summer scents and sounds.

We passed the trees of Fassefern House and the shores of Loch Eil, and ahead was an immense mountain, dark blue and untouched by cloud . . . Ben Nevis, the highest mountain in Britain. I stared in awe at the massive shoulders and wondered if we would climb to the summit one day. I knew that the cottage was right under the slopes of the Ben.

But it was the trees that held and fascinated me. The marvelous tracery of the larches, the delicate shimmer of birch leaves against the white trunks.

Only one thing drew me from the train windows, and that was the little room at the end of the corridor. I went along there more than once to wash my hands with scented soap and dry them with a clean, red-banded towel taken from the rack. The toilet had a little chain to pull; I had heard of such things, but it seemed wonderful on a *train*.

By the time we reached Fort William, I was already so filled with new impressions that I felt I could not take in any more. The station platforms were close beside Loch Linnhe, and there was a great white yacht tacking over to Argour, but I turned from natural beauty and gave all my attention to what seemed to me to be crowds of people. There was a bookstall, too, and wonderful colored posters depicting other places. There was one of the Tower of London.

"Do you think you can carry your suitcase, Mairi?" Isobel asked. "If not we'll take a taxi."

Uncle George, she had said, would not be meeting us, as he had an unbreakable rule that he always wrote from nine until at least eleven-thirty.

"Oh, yes," I said. "I want to walk, please. I want to see *everything!*"

I found that the High Street utterly bewildered me. I had never seen so many terrifying cars and motorbicycles, nor so many people. I was astonished by the number of shops and by the enormous variety of goods displayed in the windows. I stumbled along, stopping every minute or so and asking endless questions.

I must have been a great trial to Isobel, but she never showed it. The only thing that ruffled her was when I fell off the edge of the narrow sidewalk and was almost run over by a bright blue car. The driver hooted and quite obviously swore, but Isobel merely jerked me to safety and said, breathlessly, "Do be careful, Mairi! I'm responsible for you, and remember that it would be quite dull in the hospital."

After that I paid more attention to the perils of the traffic, and I was starting to feel the weight of my suitcase. I had to keep changing it from one hand to the other.

At last we were through the town and taking a narrow road that ran beside the River Nevis, which was still a white torrent in places in spite of the dry weather. There was almost no traffic, and trees arched coolly overhead. I put out my hand and touched some growing leaves. We could see the glen in front of us, green and fertile, and the immense slopes of the Ben rising across the river. Ahead were more great mountains, dim in the blue heat haze.

"I wish we could wade in the river," I said wistfully.

"Well, why not?" Isobel asked cheerfully. "We're hot and tired. Let's go down to that patch of stones."

We had been warmly clad for the night, and now all our clothes were a burden. We put down the suitcases and our coats and climbed down the grassy bank. In a few moments we were sitting side by side on a black rock, dabbling our toes cautiously in the cold mountain water. I was so happy that I started to sing, but soon Isobel said, "We'd better dry our feet and go on, Mairi. Uncle George will think we missed the train."

We walked on along the narrow, stony road, and presently, beyond a grove of thinly planted firs, we could see a small house close to the river. It was built of gray stone, and it had pointed windows and two thin chimney pots that looked like ears. It stood in a small, wild garden in which raspberry bushes ran riot. There was a small board on the gate that said: "Aconree Cottage."

"Well, here we are!" said Isobel. Then I felt her stiffen beside me. Someone was coming down the path who could not possibly be Uncle George. He seemed to be quite a young man, and he wore a bright green shirt, short-sleeved to show suntanned arms, and gray trousers that, even to me, looked shabby. They were stained with what looked like paint.

I glanced at Isobel, but she seemed quite unaware of me. She put out her hand and opened the gate. Her eyes were fixed on the advancing stranger.

"Colin!" she cried. "What on earth are *you* doing here? I thought you were in India. It can't be a coincidence—"

"Oh, I say!" he exclaimed. "You've carried your suitcases. I meant to come and meet you, but I was painting, and time passed. No, I'm not in India. I've been back for two months. And it isn't a coincidence, either. I got in touch with George, and he told me he'd rented a cottage here and you might be coming. I'm living at a house up the glen. It isn't very peaceful, though. There are seven children, so George lets me have most of my meals here. How are you, Isobel?"

"I'm fine," Isobel answered. I was sharply aware of some tension in her, and I wasn't at all pleased to see this unexpected stranger. "This is Colin Forbes-Cowan, Mairi," she said. "Colin, Mairi's a young friend of mine. . . . I expect Uncle George told you. Where *is* Uncle George?"

"Oh, he's stopped writing and he's preparing the lunch. Some special pudding . . . you know what he's like. What's the matter, Mairi?" he added. "Have I got paint on my nose? I know it's all over my trousers."

"No . . . no, indeed," I answer, confused. I had always known plenty of men, but Colin seemed quite different from any of them. His slightly sardonic glance made me shy, and I resented his presence. Isobel had never mentioned anyone called Colin Forbes-Cowan, but clearly she knew him.

"Oh, leave your suitcases. I'll carry them in," Colin said casually.

I was glad to put mine down; it seemed to weigh a ton by then. I followed Isobel up the narrow, overgrown path. The raspberry canes grasped at my bare legs and gave me several savage scratches.

"Does he paint pictures?" I whispered, as we walked around the house and came in sight of the kitchen door.

"Yes, very good pictures, Mairi. He's quite a famous artist, though he's only twenty-six. I went to an Exhibition of his work in London two years ago, and last year I met him. He was painting on the shores of Loch Lomond." I knew every tone of Isobel's voice, but I felt there was something new as she spoke. But I had little time to think then. Isobel shouted, "Uncle George! Uncle George, we're here!" and a man appeared in the kitchen doorway. Isobel had described him so often that he at once seemed familiar. There was the red and merry face, the large ears and the rather stout body that yet looked strong and vigorous. He had an absurd apron tied around his waist.

"Isobel!" he exclaimed. "It's good to see you. And is this Mairi Gilbride?"

Isobel kissed him warmly.

"Yes, this is Mairi. I think she's rather stunned by all that's happened to her."

"Did you enjoy the train?" he asked, his friendly, far-seeing eyes on my face, and I answered without much shyness. I liked and trusted Uncle George immediately.

"Oh, it was wonderful! And we had a huge breakfast in Mallaig, and that was wonderful, too."

"I hope you'll have room for some lunch."

We followed him into the kitchen, which was a dark little place, with a stone-flagged floor and a low ceiling. But it was made cheerful by a row of scarlet geraniums on the window-sill. There were cooking utensils all over the scrubbed wooden table, and a sizzling sound, as well as a delectable smell, came from the oven.

Colin went through, carrying our luggage, and his feet sounded loud on an uncovered stairway. When he came down again, he said, "I suppose I'm invited to lunch?" His tone suggested that this remark was a mere formality.

"Of course, dear boy," said Uncle George. Then he turned

125

to Isobel. "Were you surprised to find Colin here? He turned up unexpectedly two days ago."

"Very surprised," Isobel said quietly, not giving away much . . . either pleasure or dismay.

Then Uncle George led Isobel and me up the narrow stairs and took us into a large bedroom, with windows overlooking the front garden. The walls were yellow, and there was not much furniture; two small beds, a washstand with bowls and jugs on it, a dressing table, and one or two varnished chairs. To me it seemed luxurious and almost palatial after the dark partitioned space where I slept at home.

The sunlight was pouring in, and I ran to the window, leaning my elbows on the sill. The vague unease and unrest caused by the presence of Colin Forbes-Cowan was forgotten in my sudden, incredulous joy.

I was in a house on the mainland . . . I was caught up in what seemed a wild adventure. There was so much to see and do and learn.

MAIRI ON
THE MAINLAND

J ust unpack and wash, and then lunch will be ready,"
said Uncle George.

I poured ice cold mountain water into a yellow basin and
washed vigorously. It was a relief to take off my thick
clothes. Isobel sang under her breath as she unpacked her
suitcase, so maybe she had been *pleased* to see Colin.

"May I put on my red and white dress?" I asked, and she
laughed.

"Of course, if you want to."

"But it's my best."

Isobel had made the dress for me out of crisp cotton material, and I loved it.

"It will wash," she said easily.

She put on a green dress and brushed her hair until it shone. I thought we looked very grand as we went down to lunch . . . lunch! We always called it dinner, and so did Isobel when she lived with us.

The table was laid in the living room, and Uncle George carried in roast lamb and vegetables. Colin came lounging in from the garden, and the meal began. I had eaten very little meat in my life, and I thought the food even better than breakfast, but I didn't really do it justice. I kept glancing from one face to another and listening to the talk, which was lively and casual, very different from the conversations I usually heard. Colin's dark hair was untidy, and I noticed that he had high cheekbones and a very well-shaped nose. His voice had a familiar lilt, and I wondered if he were a Gaelic speaker.

Once he caught my glance and pulled a slight face at me, which made me blush.

"Lost your tongue, Mairi?" he asked, and I blushed again. "I suppose you *do* speak English?"

"Of course I am speaking English," I said, with dignity, and wished I had not used the Gaelic idiom.

I thought of Ros MacBride and how much nicer he was, even though not so handsome.

After lunch, while Isobel and I were helping to wash the dishes, she suggested that I ought to take a rest, but I was horrified by the idea.

"I'll go to bed early," I promised. "Oh, Isobel, there's so much to see. Couldn't I go back to Fort William and explore? If you want to talk to Uncle George, I'll be quite all right alone."

Isobel looked doubtful.

"Remember the traffic, Mairi."

"I will be very careful, I promise. I'm nearly thirteen . . . that's old enough to explore alone."

In the end she gave in. I could see she was longing to talk to Uncle George, sitting under the trees in the garden. Colin, it turned out, was going off to paint far up the glen.

Mother had given me some money to spend, and I dropped a shilling into the pocket of my dress. Then I set off, walking very slowly up the shadowy road. The sunlight made patterns as it fell through the leaves, and after a while, I lay down on a grassy bank and looked up at the green tracery. Trees really were a miracle.

That was a wonderful afternoon. Everything was fascinating. I looked into each store window, amazed at the variety of tartan goods on sale: rugs, scarves, ties, jackets, in every conceivable color and pattern. Buchanan, Royal Stuart, MacDonald, MacLeod. English people always seemed to like tartan, and they could clothe themselves from head to foot in it here. I saw some people who seemed to be Americans who had done just that. The men wore kilts, tartan socks, jackets and even Glengarry bonnets.

I loved to listen to the people talking. I had always been rather suspicious of tourists on the island, but here I was a tourist, too. It was a very strange thought.

I had never seen so much candy; there were whole shops simply crammed with wonderful boxes. I bought some Edinburgh rock and strolled along nibbling it.

It took me a long time to get back to the station, where I spent the rest of the afternoon. It was cool there, for a breeze was blowing from Loch Linnhe. I watched a train arrive from the South, bringing more tourists, and I stood near the booking office listening to people buying tickets. They wanted them for Glasgow, Edinburgh and even London. London seemed to me almost as far away as Canada.

When the station clock said nearly five o'clock, I thought it was time to go back to Achonree Cottage. I was halfway along the High Street when I met Isobel. She had a laden basket on her arm and said she'd been doing some shopping for Uncle George. I think she was also looking for me, because she seemed very relieved to see me.

"How was it?" she asked, as we carried the basket between us.

I told her all I had done and seen. Some of it came out in the Gaelic because I was so excited.

"And there were people buying tickets to go to London," I ended. "How do you get to London? It must be very far away."

"Yes, it is . . . several hundred miles. The train goes there," Isobel said, smiling. "The one we came on was going there. To King's Cross Station."

I was so dumbfounded by this information that I was silent for some distance. Then Isobel said she had bought some stamps and some picture postcards and we would sit by the river and write them. I wrote one to Jean, one to Mother and one to Ros MacBride. It was hard to fit in all I wanted to say. We dropped them into a mailbox at the side of the road.

The early evening was golden and beautiful as we strolled on to Achonree. I remembered Colin and wondered if he would be back for supper. I hoped not.

"Are artists poor?" I asked suddenly. Colin *looked* poor— his shirt had been torn and his trousers were awful, but he didn't sound poor, somehow. He had such an air of assurance.

Isobel laughed.

"Some are very poor, but if you're thinking of Colin he certainly isn't. For one thing he had a very quick success. I believe his first exhibition was four years ago, and his work caught on at once. He was soon getting good prices." She was silent for a moment, then said, as though half to herself, "He might have been better if he'd had to struggle a bit."

"Is it good to struggle? It isn't nice being poor." The news that Colin had money didn't seem good somehow. Ros must have hardly any; he had a tiny piece of land and ran the mail-boat. But he had told us he was writing a book about Celtic languages and literature. Maybe that would be a great success and make him rich.

Isobel was frowning. "Sometimes it doesn't hurt to have to fight for something, Mairi. Colin's had everything much too easy, and he thinks he can get everything that way. His father was a schoolteacher in the Highlands . . . up in Ross-shire, I believe. He wrote a bit, and when he was around thirty he gave up teaching and went to London. Colin told me the tale last year. He made a precarious living as a writer and freelance journalist. Colin's mother was Welsh; a Gwynedd Evans from Snowdonia. They had a hard time for a couple of years, then an uncle of his father's died in New Zealand. He had emigrated there as a young man and made a lot of money, and it all came to his nephew. So Colin doesn't remember being poor. He was well-educated and then went to Paris to study art. His father and mother are dead now, and Colin owns a place in Wales and a small farm in Rossshire. His best pictures are the Welsh ones, I think, but he's always wandering around."

I rather hoped that Colin would soon decide to go to Africa. He must like Isobel or he wouldn't have come to Glen Nevis. If she married anyone, I did so want it to be Ros. But

I couldn't worry about it for long on that enchanted summer evening with the light so golden on the slopes of the Ben.

Isobel made me go up to bed the moment I had finished my supper, and I was yawning by then and couldn't hide the fact that I was sleepy. Colin arrived just as I had my foot on the bottom stair, and Uncle George said there was plenty of cold meat and apple pie if he was hungry.

I *was* sleepy, but I lay for quite a long while listening to the roar of the river as it fell over rocks near the cottage and the late twittering of the birds. It seemed strange to hear small birds instead of seagulls. Presently I heard voices in the garden and crept cautiously out of bed to see Isobel and Colin sitting on the wall. But she came upstairs quite soon, and then I did fall asleep.

On the whole I didn't see much of Colin Forbes-Cowan. He usually had his breakfast at the farm where he was staying, and most often he was out painting all day. Sometimes he was at Achonree for supper, and afterward he and Isobel might stroll along the road together, but she didn't seem to seek or particularly desire his company, and I felt a good deal reassured.

Life really was a succession of miracles. For days the mere fact of living in a two-storied house was remarkable. The stairs were dark, and I often fell up or down them. Uncle George pretended to be really worried. He said I was bent on breaking all my bones so that I wouldn't have to go home.

I liked Uncle George more every day. I loved to watch him cooking; he was so neat and hardly ever spilled anything. And the astonishing variety of the food was certainly a miracle.

Isobel and I went for several excursions. We took a steamer

trip down to Oban one day, and I was thrilled to see a bigger town than Fort William. We went to Fort Augustus by bus, and I saw the great Benedictine Abbey there and watched the paddle steamers going through the locks on the Caledonian Canal. And one day we climbed Ben Nevis to the very top. Uncle George went with us, and I was amazed at how easily he endured the long, terribly rough track. It was wonderful to stand on top of the world.

The weather was mostly glorious. There was only one wet and misty day, and then, of course, Colin couldn't paint. He had finished his picture of Glen Nevis and was working a few miles away at Glenfinnan. He idled away the hours at Achonree, in such a mood of heavy gloom that I was rather shocked, and Isobel seemed irritated with him.

"He's frustrated," Uncle George whispered to me, when I came in from a wet scramble by the river. "He usually gets what he wants, and what he wants right now is a blue sky and everything clear and brilliant."

When the sun shone again, Isobel and I went all the way to Inverness, passing through Fort Augustus and along the shores of Loch Ness. So I saw a real city, with a castle and cathedrals. It was a wonderful thrill, but the thing that amazed me most was the glimpses I had in the Great Glen of huge fields of ripening oats and wheat. I had never imagined farming could be like that. I thought of the tiny, tiny patches on the island, and my heart contracted with a kind of pain and a definite stab of homesickness. How hard life was for everyone I knew.

I never forgot about seeing Jean, of course, and Isobel kept her promise. One evening, when we had been in Glen Nevis for a week, she and I walked into Fort William to telephone to Glasgow. I had never spoken to anyone on the telephone, and I was shivering with nervous incredulity as I stood beside Isobel. She gave the number and put in the money and then she spoke to someone . . . Mrs. Robertson. Isobel explained who she was and said she hoped Jean could have a day off to meet us somewhere. Maybe Crianlarich would be a good place. We could each go by train and have a few hours together.

Then Jean was called to the telephone and, after greeting her, Isobel handed the receiver to me.

"Just speak slowly and clearly, Mairi, and Jean will hear you," she said.

"I—I can't!" I gasped, and I heard Jean laugh. "Oh, Isobel, she heard me! Jean, it's Mairi."

Then I heard Jean's voice, soft and sweet and unbearably familiar, as if she were with us, and not many miles away in Glasgow. I wanted to say so much, but I could only gasp out a few sentences. I spoke in the Gaelic, which still came easiest in times of stress.

Isobel took the receiver again and fixed the meeting with Jean, for she had looked up the times of trains in advance.

I walked back to Glen Nevis in a daze. Only one thing was clear. I owed everything to Isobel. I looked at her suntanned face, framed in soft, fair hair, very smooth above her low brow and curling a little around her ears. She was swinging a green sweater and she wore a yellow dress. Suddenly I knew I terribly wanted her to be happy, but I still hoped she wouldn't want to marry Colin.

The night before we met Jean, I couldn't sleep. I lay gazing at the starry sky for hours on end, remembering the time when Jean had left home. It seemed so long ago. I had been only a child then, knowing nothing.

At sunrise Isobel awoke and stared at me.

"What is it, Mairi?"

"It's Jean," I whispered. "She didn't sound so very different on the telephone, but I—I am almost scared to see her again. What shall I do if she isn't the same?"

"She'll still be Jean," Isobel said comfortingly. "Fatter, you know, and more than a year older. You needn't be scared. She won't have changed all that much."

I was still scared when we left, and I didn't really enjoy the train journey, even though I was going south and seeing a lot of new country. We reached Crianlarich first, and I could hardly keep still. It was a small station, with flowers, and the air was sweet and warm. I might not have noticed if it had been snowing.

Then Jean's train arrived, and I saw her smooth, dark head at a window. She jumped out and ran to us, flushed, eager and almost tearful. I clung to her, talking incoherently, and it was some time before I stood back and really looked at her. She was different in a way, but Isobel had been right . . . she was still Jean. She wasn't cheaply smart and red-lipped like some of the girls who came home. She wore a neat blue coat and a blue and white cotton dress and carried a real grown-up handbag.

Her face was much fuller, and, even when her first excitement had died down, it was still pink. She looked healthy and well-fed, and her hair shone. The cut was much better than Mother had ever achieved.

That day was a mixture of happiness and sorrow. I don't think I took my eyes off Jean's face for very long. Something in my heart that had seemed to die when Jean went away was alive and warm again. It was that feeling of peace, warmth and safety that only her presence had ever brought.

We climbed up into the hills and sat on the hot grass to eat the picnic lunch Uncle George had provided. The cries of the sheep seemed slow and sleepy in the sunny air, and all around rose the mountains of Perthshire. And how we talked! Sometimes in English, but more often in the Gaelic, which of course Isobel could speak fluently by then. We told her every scrap of news about Glen Gaoth, and Jean told us about her life in Glasgow and stressed Mrs. Robertson's kindness.

"She treats me almost as one of the family," she said. "In a few days we're going to stay in the North of England. Imagine that, Mairi! You never thought I should see England, did you?"

"But when are you coming home? It's nearly fifteen months since you went away."

"In the early autumn," said Jean. "Mrs. Robertson says she will pay my fare. Oh, Mairi, how I long to be back on the island! To see everyone . . . Mother and Uilleam Angus and Ros."

There was such deep longing in her voice that I was wholly reassured. She didn't want to stay in the great city of Glasgow forever.

We lay stretched out on the grass, hearing the gurgling flow of a burn. In repose Jean's face looked older and much prettier; her body was more mature, though she was still small and slight.

Later we spent a long time picking early wild raspberries. They were very sweet and delicious. Then we had tea in a cottage garden and Jean insisted on paying for it. Isobel didn't argue, for anyone could see that Jean was proud to have money in her purse. It was then that I noticed her very charming dignity; she was still shy, quiet and sweet, but her head was well-poised and her manner assured. Yes, certainly Jean had "learned" in Glasgow.

The parting was almost unbearable, but somehow I managed not to cry or hold her too long. Jean herself stood very straight, waving until our train carried us away. Hers would take her south very soon.

I sat in silence until we passed Bridge of Orchy, staring out the window with a pain at my heart and behind my eyes. Isobel read a book and left me alone until I burst out, "Why does Jean have to be away from home? It isn't fair!"

"No, in many ways it isn't fair," Isobel agreed quietly. "But then life hardly ever is, Mairi. And it's done her no harm; you can see that for yourself."

"Oh, I know that," I mumbled. "She has a good time. She's going to England, and she loves the Robertson children. She borrows books out of a great library, and she goes to classes at night. I meant . . . I meant that *I* want Jean."

"And she wants you. She wants to be at home with you and your mother. But Jean made up her mind to be independent, and she's making the best of things."

"I—maybe she's lucky, Isobel," I said slowly. For in the past week or two I had learned much about the joys of the mainland. "Maybe it's right to leave the island."

"It's inevitable, anyway, for some people," Isobel said, a little sadly. "Some day you'll leave it yourself, Mairi."

I stared at her, not quite so shocked as I would have been even a short time before.

"How could I? I . . . I live there, with Mother. It's my *home,* Isobel."

"I know, dear. But no one knows what will happen. You said once that you wanted to help the islands. If you're to do that, you'll first have to go away. Because you must be educated, and the school can't do anything for you after you're fourteen. No, I don't know what will happen. Don't look at me like that. You have brains, and you can't be held back. There'll be a way."

"Everything comes to an end," I said. "Everyone goes away! The boys and Jean and the old woman went away. I hate change, because it means that nothing's safe."

"Nothing *is* safe," Isobel agreed. I had hoped she would deny it. "But things are good while they last, Mairi, and there's always something new and exciting. You're learning something all the time, aren't you?"

"Yes," I said. "And you came when Jean went away."

She smiled very kindly.

"And there'll be other people, other experiences. You're going to do a lot of things, Mairi."

"I wish I knew what sort of things."

"You'll find out. Don't be unhappy."

"I'm not," I said. "I'm not. But it was awful saying good-bye to Jean for a second time."

CROFTER'S
CHILD

The days passed very quickly after that. There was only one week left. We did the housework, helped Uncle George with the cooking when he'd let us, and discovered new places of interest in the neighborhood. Uncle George wrote every morning, and then he wasn't to be disturbed. He was writing a serial called *I Loved You Once,* and sometimes he discussed the plot with Isobel and they argued and even laughed. I was rather puzzled by Uncle George's writing. It seemed quite different from Isobel's *Hebridean Year* or the very serious work Ros was planning. When I asked Uncle George if he liked writing his serials and short stories, he laughed.

"Mairi, I intended to be a serious novelist, but it wasn't in me. I can do this very well, and my stories please people and bring in enough money to make life moderately pleasant. I'm a hack. Have you ever heard that term? What I write is not great literature, but there's a demand for it that I can supply."

Each evening Colin and Isobel sat out on the wall or walked up and down the glen road. Uncle George and I, left alone after supper, would make toffee or wonderful pink and white candy until the midges drove Colin and Isobel indoors. Colin never wore another pair of trousers. He always wore the shabby, paint-stained gray ones and an old colored shirt, bright green or pink or yellow. When it was cold, he wore an old tweed jacket. He was very tall and, beside him, Isobel looked smaller and neater than ever.

Colin even wore those clothes when he took Isobel out to tea at the grandest hotel in Fort William on our next to last afternoon.

That same evening I was sitting on the wall by the gate when he strolled up and sat down beside me.

"What are you thinking about all alone, Mairi?"

"Nothing," I answered. I always feared that he was laughing at me.

"Well, I want to ask you something . . . a favor. It's an idea I had as soon as I saw you—"

At that moment Uncle George appeared around the house, waving an orange, and I slid thankfully off the wall.

"Uncle George wants me," I said, and ran off. I didn't much want to do Colin a favor, though I couldn't imagine what it might be.

But on our very last afternoon I was alone in the High Street when I came face to face with Colin. He was carrying his painting materials and must have come off the train from

Glenfinnan.

"Well, hello!" he cried, looking pleased. "How would you like some lemonade? It's appallingly hot!"

I shook my head as we stood close together on the sidewalk. I was so close to him I had to look up to see his face.

"Well, strawberry ice cream, then?"

"No, thank you!" I said, but my voice lacked conviction.

"There's a place right here," Colin said, and led the way into a very small restaurant, with green-topped tables. I felt terribly shy and awkward and rather annoyed with myself because I had given in so easily. I wished I hadn't met Colin, and I wished that the ice cream would come quickly so that I would have something to do.

"I told you I wanted to ask a favor of you," Colin said cheerfully. "But Uncle George tempted you with an orange."

I wanted to say that I had left him on purpose and that the orange had had nothing to do with it. But I was much too shy.

"Why don't you like me, Mairi?" Colin asked.

I stared at him. He was smiling in his most charming way, and I realized that I *did* like him in a way. He was very interesting.

"I—I have never met anyone like you before."

"No, poor kid!" he said, amused. "I bet you haven't. All those hard-working crofters. They're fine men. Make no mistake; I know many in Rosshire and their counterparts in Wales. I came from that kind of stock. My grandfather on my father's side was a crofter."

The ice cream came then, enormous lumps of it on pink plates to match.

"I don't see how I can be doing you a favor," I said, wielding my spoon.

"Do you think your mother would let me paint you?" he asked.

I dropped the spoon with a clatter on the table. Colin picked it up and handed it back to me.

"I'd like to paint you at the door of your croft-house with that dog, Ruari, I've heard about."

"Ruari? Paint *me*? But—Oh, but—" I took a gulp of strawberry ice cream and nearly choked. I had thought, and rather hoped, that we would never see Colin again, and now here he was wanting to come to the Outer Isles. "But where would you live?"

"There's a hotel, isn't there?"

"Not in Glen Gaoth." I was bewildered, but did know that I wasn't going to suggest him staying with the Beaths.

"There's one over the loch in Alvadale, isn't there?"

"Oh, but . . . Uilleam Angus would be charging you ten shillings every time he brought you over."

"Never mind about that," said Colin, laughing, and I said sulkily, "I forgot you were rich."

"If I come, will your mother let me paint you, Mairi?"

"No," I said. "There is much work to be done when school finishes. Isobel and I both help my mother. She's all alone, you know. It's very hard without a man. You ought to know that."

"But I'll pay you to sit for me, you know."

I was overawed at the idea of being painted and actually being paid money, but still I hesitated. Dimly I knew that he wanted to see Isobel again and was using me as a kind of excuse.

"How much would you pay me?" I asked, and he laughed with what seemed real amusement.

"Enough to make it worthwhile. You could buy all kinds

of things. Chocolate and new dresses. . . ."

I looked at him as severely as I could.

"I am not wanting to be painted, but if I earned any money I would give most of it to my mother and buy *books* with the rest. I love new dresses, but I need new books more. But have you asked Isobel?"

"No," he said, looking disconcerted. "Why should I?"

"Well, I'm with her. She's responsible for me. You should ask her first."

I spooned up the last of the ice cream and prepared to go. Colin leaned across the table.

"Be a sport, Mairi! I do want to paint you, but I want to see Isobel again as well. And I'm not sure that she wants to see me."

We stared at each other. I thought of Ros and how wonderful it would be if Isobel stayed in the Isles forever.

"You must ask Isobel. Thank you very much for the ice cream. I must go now. I have to pack my suitcase." And I ran almost all the way to the cottage. I was there long before Colin.

When he came, he was so clearly "in a mood" that Isobel looked at him in surprise.

"What's the matter? The light's been perfect all day."

"If you want to know, I asked Mairi if I could come to the Isles and paint her. But she doesn't seem very keen. She said I must ask you."

I stole away down the back garden to the river, wondering if I had done wrong to refuse to be painted. I kicked off my sandals and sat on a boulder, dangling my feet in the water. Gradually it dawned on me that Colin had paid me a compliment. He was a famous artist, after all. He had two reasons for wanting to come to the Isles, but still he wouldn't suggest painting me unless he really wanted to. He could have painted Isobel herself, but he had chosen me.

Isobel found me there on the rocks a while later.

"Mairi," she began, "I've told him we will ask your mother."

"Do you want him to come?" I mumbled, and she answered, "Maybe. I wish I really knew, Mairi."

"Then, if you do, I will let him paint me," I said.

"It might be a wonderful picture, Mairi. Think . . . it might even be hung in the Royal Academy in London."

So, when we left Achonree Cottage the next morning, Isobel carried a letter to Mother from Colin Forbes-Cowan. We carried also, crammed into our suitcases, a number of presents.

I looked around the yellow bedroom with regret, knowing that our house would seem poky and dark. I took a last chocolate cookie from the tin on the kitchen shelf and thought rather sadly of oatcakes and herrings.

Colin and Uncle George walked with us to the station. It was a great honor that Uncle George should leave his work. We were rather late and had to rush along the High Street; there was no time for a last look at the posters or the book-stall. They pushed us into the train a few moments before it left. Uncle George shook hands with me and left some money in my palm. Isobel kissed him through the open window and told him to take care of himself. Colin and Isobel didn't seem to say good-bye properly. He just said, "Well, I hope Mrs. Gilbride will agree. If she does, I'll be over in not more than three weeks' time." To me he added, "Well, good-bye to you, Mairi. Mind you aren't sick during the crossing."

"I am not likely to be sick," I said, with great dignity.

"He's only teasing," said Isobel.

Colin walked rapidly beside the moving train.

"The trouble with you, Mairi, is that you have no sense of humor."

He was right, I suppose. I took everything very seriously, but then the issue was quite a serious one.

"*You* never tease," I said to Isobel. Then I stood alone in the corridor, watching Fort William for as long as I could. And when we were past Corpach and were speeding along the shores of Loch Eil, there was the great bulk of Ben Nevis, with not one cloud on the summit. It was a great satisfaction to remember that I had stood on the very top.

In a few days the sharpness of my memories had faded a trifle, but I looked across the Minch from Ulval with understanding and knowledge. School had not finished, and I found that I had acquired a new status there since I had been to the mainland. For some time afterward I had an audience eager to hear of my experiences.

One of the best things about coming home was seeing Mother again. She was on the rocks waiting for us, wrapped in her shawl against the chilly wind. At first she looked at me wonderingly and doubtfully, as if expecting me to be different. I certainly felt very different, but by the time we had had supper and unpacked the presents, the holiday was already almost dreamlike.

Mother read Colin's letter and at first shook her head.

"Why will he want to be painting Mairi? She is only a child still and has no fine clothes."

Isobel explained that Colin wanted to paint me outside the house with Ruari and that he would pay me well enough to buy strong shoes for the winter and many other things. Mother was no fool, though she had spent so many years in

Glen Gaoth. She thought for a long time.

"This Mr. Forbes-Cowan will be a famous artist?"

"Yes, he's very well-known. And he's only twenty-six."

"And London people will see the picture?"

"Yes. It might even be hung in the Royal Academy," Isobel told her.

In the end Mother made a stipulation that I didn't really understand.

"If he is wishing, he can come here and paint Mairi. But tell him that he must not, for any reason, say who the girl in the picture is or where she will be living. We will be glad of the money, and we will be making him very welcome, but London people are not to know it is Mairi Gilbride of Glen Gaoth."

Isobel agreed, but I felt faintly disappointed. Why shouldn't people know it was Mairi Gilbride? I think I felt that there ought to be some compensation for letting Colin come to the island.

He arrived without warning one evening nearly three weeks later. Isobel was weaving, and I was hunched up on my stool, reading, with my feet nearly on the hearth, for the weather had turned gray and cold. Mother was sitting beside me, knitting.

Suddenly Ruari growled, and someone passed the window. I only caught a glimpse of bluish tweed, for the window was very tiny and set deep in the wall. Then there was a knock at the door, and Mother said, "See who it is, Mairi."

So I went to open the door, with my hand on Ruari's bristling fur, and there stood Colin. I said "Oh!" and stared blankly.

Colin laughed in a friendly way and said, "Hello, Mairi! I wondered if I'd found the right place."

"Will you be coming in?" I asked, with dignity, though annoyed that my good English had deserted me.

Isobel had heard his voice and came around the partition to greet him, and Mother put the kettle hastily on to the glowing peats.

Colin was actually wearing another pair of trousers, and his shirt was white under his tweed jacket. His faced seemed browner and his eyes greener than I remembered, and his hair was ruffled. He was very polite to Mother, and I knew that she liked him. He sat drinking tea, his long legs spread out, and answered her questions. Yes, the crossing had been rough. The hotel seemed as if it would be comfortable. Yes, it was crowded just now.

Presently I went on with my reading, though I knew it was rude. I just didn't know what to say to Colin. Once I looked up and his gaze was fixed on me.

"What are you reading, Mairi?" he asked.

"She will be very bad-mannered to have her nose in a book when there is a guest," said Mother.

"Poetry," I said.

"Oh! Is it school work? A vacation task?"

"It's Celtic poetry," said Isobel. "The poetry they read in school doesn't amount to much. Ros MacBride, who gave me Gaelic lessons last winter, is lending her his books, and Father Donald does the same. She's insatiable."

"Clever, eh? So what's going to happen to her?"

"We don't know yet," Isobel said quietly.

We left the unguessable future—though the subject returned to my mind disturbingly later—and Colin began to discuss the picture. We all went outside, and I felt reluctant, vaguely important and resentful all at once. Colin walked up and down on the hard mud, scaring the hens and drawing curious glances from Alan Beath, who was sitting smoking outside his house.

You would never have thought to see the drab landscape, palely glowing here and there with patches of ripening corn, that it could be flooded with brilliant color. Behind us the glen was purple with bell heather, but the heavy sky failed to draw color from it.

Colin stared down at the *clachan* and the loch, and he and Isobel talked about light and background. I felt cold and rather unhappy, for Colin's arrival had spoiled a pleasant evening. His advent seemed to have taken Isobel right away from us into his world. There she was, wearing a scarlet sweater and a gray skirt, walking up and down and looking very small beside him.

That evening Colin was more pleasant and charming than he had ever seemed in Glen Nevis, and he looked different without his bright shirt and old trousers.

Presently Isobel went down to the shore with him, and Mother sent me to bed, saying that it was late and I looked tired. I went without protest, but I couldn't sleep for a long time. I was terribly afraid that Isobel would marry Colin and I felt it would be so much better if it were Ros.

The next day was as gray as the preceding one and very misty. Isobel said Colin had to have sunshine for the picture, and of course the weather would annoy him. He didn't appear all day, but Isobel had arranged to have dinner with him at the hotel that evening.

So when she went down to ask Uilleam Angus to take her across the loch, I set off to visit Ros MacBride. I had not been to his house for quite a while, though he had been to see us several times since our return. He had been there the very night after we came home. He wanted to know all about Jean, and we told him in detail. Then he and Isobel had plunged into one of their usual discussions and had seemed so happy together that I had almost forgotten Colin.

Now Colin had arrived, and Isobel was away across the loch to have dinner with him, and I had a sudden longing to see Ros. Peggy MacKay had wanted me to go down to Arbhar, but I preferred to tramp the bleak miles to Polleray.

Aunt Morag was taking in some clean clothes from the grassy bank behind the house. I heard her coughing when I was still some distance away. She looked very small and as neat as ever in her black dress. She was still coughing when I reached her, but she managed to greet me.

"It is long since I was seeing you, Mairi! You look cold, *caileag*. Run into the house . . . there will be a good fire." Her small face was anxious, as usual, and her thin shoulders shook as she coughed again.

"Why don't you wear a shawl?" I asked, rather timidly.

"Oh, a shawl will be a cumbersome garment. I could never work in a shawl." She fumbled with the clean clothes and dropped them and I helped to pick them up. "My cough is nothing . . . nothing at all. Ros was saying the doctor would give me something, but it will soon be better."

I followed her into the house, vaguely disturbed. I had once heard Mother say, "Morag MacBride will be catching her death there on that cold shore and she never warmly clad."

"Death" was a frightening word. People did die. The *cailleach* had died, and old Jenny Campbell; and Sorcha MacDonald was very ill, they said.

Aunt Morag bustled me into the living room. She piled another peat on the blaze, tripped over a stool, and went away, still coughing. Ros had been working at the table, but he pushed aside his papers and greeted me kindly. He was still wearing his great boots and his face had a red, cold look. He said he had not long returned from Glascreagh. He had taken the doctor across, and it was true old Sorcha was dying.

I sat down and accepted a slab of chocolate.

"And what's the matter with you, Mairi?" Ros asked. "You look gloomy."

"Colin Forbes-Cowan has come," I told him. "But he couldn't start his picture today because there was no sun. And now Isobel has gone across the loch to have dinner with him."

Ros had already heard about the meeting with Colin on the mainland, and how he might come to paint my portrait, so it was no surprise to him. But I watched his face curiously to see if he minded about Isobel.

He didn't seem to, for his face remained quite placid, and he said, "Well, Isobel will enjoy that. I believe they do a very good dinner over there."

Oh, if *only* Ros loved Isobel! If only he'd show some emotion. But he was asking me about the picture and how I felt now that Colin had come.

"You'll have to sit very still, I suppose. You may not like that. He sounds a slightly temperamental chap. I dare say most artists are. It will take patience, Mairi."

"He's going to call it 'Crofter's Child,' " I said. "And that's what I am."

"It's nothing to be ashamed of, is it? Your father was a fine man. I knew him when I was a boy."

"No, I am not ashamed," I said quickly. "Colin's own grandfather was a crofter; he told me that. But look where Colin's got to. He's rich and famous and he. . . . I think he always gets what he wants. And what will happen to me? Next summer I'll be fourteen. You once said you'd help me, Ros, but what can I *do* to get properly educated? I'll have to earn money, won't I? Neill sends us a little, but Martin has never sent any money at all. Mother won't talk to me about it, but I think Martin should send something, even though his wife is going to have a baby. If Isobel leaves us, we will have very little, and Mother works so hard . . . too hard. It frightens me sometimes, in case she should be sick."

Ros had lit his pipe and was puffing thoughtfully. After a few moments he said slowly:

"I shouldn't worry too much, Mairi. I will try and help you when a way shows itself, for I think there's real work for you to do when you're older. But it seems to me that you will be able to help yourself. You've grown into such a fine girl, and you're learning all the time. I know Isobel has helped a great deal."

"Isobel. . . . Oh, I owe nearly everything to her."

"You've been with her almost daily for nearly a year and a half. But she *won't* stay forever, Mairi."

"I know," I whispered, and looked down. "But she'll always stay our friend, won't she?"

"I'm sure she will. She's been a real friend to you."

As I walked the rough road home from Polleray, I thought over the conversation. I was a crofter's child . . . a crofter's girl. I didn't see the future in any way clear, but *somehow* I would make a success of my life. In spite of the cold and the gathering twilight, I had a sudden moment of hope and joy. I was sure that all would be well.

SECOND
SIGHT?

When I reached home, there was a letter from Jean that Uilleam Angus had brought across the loch. Mother had left it for me to open. I read it rapidly, not aloud.

"Oh!" I gasped. "She really is coming, Mother! During the first week in September. Mrs. Robertson is paying her fare, and she will be staying two weeks." I found that my eyes were full of tears and my voice shook. All my memories of Jean crowded back into my mind; all my pain at our recent parting.

"Well, *mo chridhe,* is that cause for tears?" Mother asked, but her own eyes did not seem to me quite dry.

"No," I said, sobbing. "No. But I want her so much."

Mother sighed and smiled, then she took me in her arms,

a very unusual gesture.

"I am wanting her, too. It seems so long since she went away."

By the time Isobel returned, flushed, cold and bright-eyed, we were happy and elated. It was very late, and I was already washed and in my nightgown. But first we had to tell Isobel the good news, and then we had to hear about the dinner.

"Did you have lovely food?" I asked. "Tell us exactly what you had."

"Soup, and fish and roast chicken, Mairi. And meringue and cream, with cherries on top. And afterward there was a concert in the lounge. Colin sang Welsh songs, and I sang the songs from our book. Then we all sang together. They were mostly English people . . . sportsmen. Colin's opinion is that only fools enjoy shooting and fishing."

"I've often heard Colin say that people are fools," I said.

"So he does! It's rather a habit of his."

"But this time he is right. People should only do those things when they're hungry, not for the fun of it. Is he coming to paint me tomorrow?"

"Yes, in the morning if the sun shines."

The next day was fine and warm, with brilliant color everywhere. Colin came across the loch very early, carrying his easel and painting materials. In his old clothes he looked more like the Colin of Glen Nevis, and seemed more like him, too. This was his work mood. He looked at the lovely lights and shadows on the hills and water and grunted with satisfaction. I felt rather shaky and scared and hung around the doorway. Mother kept pulling at my old skirt and running a comb through my hair.

"Indeed and fancy wanting to paint you in that old red

jersey, when you could be wearing the new dress Isobel was making for you!"

"She's fine as she is," Colin said brusquely. "But I want her hair untidy, and she can take off those sandals. Bare brown feet ... that's better."

Isobel sat sewing in the heather at a distance. She understood very well that Colin didn't want close company. Her job, she had been told, was to keep people away, if anyone showed curiosity.

Colin took me by the arm and made me sit down on the stone by the door. Then he made me alter my position four or five times until he was satisfied. His manner was sharp and absorbed, and he didn't seem to care if I was comfortable. Ros had been right; I wasn't going to enjoy having my portrait painted. But I was being paid for it, and I must just endure the boredom of sitting still.

Colin, satisfied at last, began to work. After a very short time I longed to move; I longed to look the other way toward the *clachan*. After what seemed hours I got a cramp in my foot and grimaced so much that Colin asked irritably, "What's the matter? Is something biting you?"

"No," I said coldly. I sat staring at his absorbed brown face, feeling increasingly bored. I wanted to read or have Isobel talk to me. But presently she rose and went up to the Beaths' house, and Colin and I were left alone. Mother was busy indoors.

Sometimes people passed close by on the track, but they were too polite to come near and stare. The news had got around that a famous artist was painting me, and it was a nine days' wonder, but Islesfolk have good manners. Colin needn't have been afraid that they would breathe over his shoulder.

154

After what seemed to me a lifetime of holding the one position, Colin told me to stretch my legs for five minutes. I stretched and groaned and ran thankfully away.

The sittings varied very little. The weather stayed warm, clear and blue, so Colin was in a very good mood; but he seemed to think I could keep still forever. Sometimes, when he was working on the background, I was free, but I always had to stay within call. I *longed* to go to Arbhar with Peggy MacKay and wade in the rock pools, but I could only do that in the evenings. The only compensation was that all the other young people regarded me with awe, because I was having my portrait painted. Colin wouldn't even let me see the picture until it was finished, and I knew it was no good arguing, though I was curious to see the result of all those hours and days of absorbed work.

Isobel and Colin spent every evening together. They borrowed bicycles and rode over to the Atlantic shore and bathed in the shallow green water. I thought that rather a strange thing to do. I liked to wade in the rock pools, but I had never immersed myself in the ocean.

I felt rather lonely and left out, and I longed for the portrait to be finished.

One morning I met Colin in the *clachan* when he had just come over the loch. He was carrying a parcel and gave it to me.

"Some chocolates for you, Mairi. You may be glad to know that the picture will be finished in a day or two. You haven't enjoyed it, have you?"

I took the chocolates and gazed up at him. He was smiling.

"It's very dull having one's portrait painted," I said. "And you won't even let me see it."

"You'll see it soon. You shall have a first view, of course;

but it's going to be shown in the school here for a day, so that everyone can come and look at it. Father Donald has the key, and I've fixed it with him."

"Really?" That sounded rather exciting.

Colin took my arm and led me up the hill.

"And I haven't thanked you, Mairi. You've been a good lass . . . very patient. I'm pleased with the picture; I hope it's a good one."

That was Colin at his very nicest, using all his charm. When he was like that, I almost thought Isobel could be happy with him. Though she didn't seem particularly happy at the moment. Sometimes she was surprisingly irritable.

When at last I saw the picture, it gave me a violent, nameless pleasure. It made my heart sing and my tongue silent. It seemed like a miracle that it was I there on the canvas. That girl with the suntanned, pointed face, the red lips and soft black hair could not be Mairi Gilbride! There was pride in the face, and thoughtfulness. I stared for a long, long time at that little figure on the stone seat.

Colin had painted the picture so that the house was at the side, and the *clachan,* the loch and the distant hills made a background. You could almost believe that the stones of our house were real, and Ruari looked real, too. He had been a better sitter than I . . . he'd seemed to know exactly what was required of him.

At last I said, "I am glad you painted it. Will people in London really see it?"

"I hope so, Mairi," Colin said. "But I don't intend to sell it for a long time."

"And London people won't know who that girl is?"

"No. I promised your mother. People might come here to see you. She wouldn't like that."

So that had been why Mother had made that strange stipulation. My nearness to fame made me silent again. People to come across the Minch to see *me!*

Hundreds of people came to the school to view the picture. It was more exciting than a wedding or a funeral. But it was only local people. The tourists in the hotel knew nothing about it. They only rarely crossed the loch to our lonely shore.

Ros came and met Colin for the first time, and I was surprised that they seemed to get on so well. They spoke Welsh together, and Ros seemed delighted to have a chance to practice the language.

Then the picture was packed up, ready to be taken to London, and Colin's last day came. In the evening Isobel went over the loch to see him off on the steamer.

It sailed late, as usual, and I was in bed, but far from asleep, when she returned. I had been thinking thankfully that now Colin had gone and we could return to normal.

Isobel talked to Mother for a short while, then slipped around the partition. When she sensed that I was not asleep, she sat down on my bed.

"Well, he's gone, Mairi!" she whispered.

"Yes," I whispered back, and waited, with an instinct that more was to come. She took my hand and held it for a moment.

"He asked me to marry him," she murmured, and my heart leaped with fear and excitement. But I said nothing, and she went on, "He wanted us to marry almost at once; then I could go to Italy with him. He's going for the whole winter. But I said no, not yet. I—maybe I am beginning to love him, but I'm not sure. And I want to stay here for a few more months. I'm going to write a novel about a croft-

157

ing family, and I must write it here."

"Oh, Isobel!" I whispered. A few more months . . . the winter. Anything was better than nothing. "If you married him would . . . would he make you happy?"

"I don't know," said Isobel. "Perhaps not, all the time. But I might try and make *him* happy. He's talented and rich, but unsettled, and. . . . Oh, I don't know."

"I—I was so hoping it would be Ros," I confessed, and she jumped.

"Ros is a good friend, Mairi. He's a fine man. But we never thought of being in love. Ros . . . I think he has other plans. Other hopes, at least."

"But who can Ros marry if not you?" I wailed.

"That's his secret, for the present. Ros will be all right, I think; and I. . . . Well, we'll forget it for a while, shall we? Jean's coming soon, and I shall write my book."

She crept away into her own corner of the house, and I curled up, feeling at least more peaceful. The next few months were safe, anyway, and Jean *would* be coming soon.

We all went across the loch to meet Jean; we were on the pier much too early. I had eaten very little that day and my legs felt weak. I was cold, too, though it was a warm enough evening.

I thought that the steamer would never come, but at last it came creeping into the loch from the great darkening stretch of the Minch. The ship was blazing with lights, and at last we saw Jean on deck. Then, as soon as she could, she ran down the gangplank into our arms.

"Oh, Mother! Mairi! Isobel!" she cried. "I *can't* believe I'm really home again. Oh, how good to smell the peat smoke and the heather and to see the island again!"

"So you have not learned the wrong things?" Mother

said at last, staring at her searchingly, and Jean met her eyes unflinchingly. Jean *was* changed, but it was for the better, in every way.

"Mrs. Robertson wouldn't have liked it," said Jean.

"Praise her for her good sense!" said Mother.

Then many people began to greet Jean, and suddenly Ros MacBride came striding on to the pier. Everyone fell back, for Ros was well-respected. He took Jean's hands and looked down at her.

"So you've come back? It's a good day for us all!"

"But what is the matter, Ros?" Mother was staring at him, and my heart suddenly gave a great jump. Yes, something was the matter! Ros looked harassed and tired.

"It's Aunt Morag," he said. "You know she's had a cough for a long time and wouldn't see the doctor? She grew worse yesterday, and I sent for him. This morning she was taken to the hospital, and I have just been along there." The hospital was a small building half a mile outside Alvadale.

Cold fear made my stomach feel terrible again, and I forgot the happiness of Jean's arrival. I saw the bleak shore and the gray sea and the old woman gathering the clean clothes in her arms. I remembered how she had coughed and how I had thought of death.

Then everything went dark. I had forgotten Jean, but suddenly I heard her voice crying, "Mairi, what is it? Are you ill?"

I still didn't see her very clearly.

"I—I was thinking. It is wild. I can hear the wind, and it's very cold. Aunt Morag will die. She is dead. There is a yellow sunset . . . gold all over the sky. Aunt Morag is dead!"

"Mairi, what are you saying?" Jean's voice was sharp. I opened my eyes—or at least they cleared—to see inquiring, anxious faces and the bustle around the steamer.

"I don't know," I said, trembling and icy cold. But I remembered the words I had spoken as if they had been said by someone else.

"The child has the second sight!" said Mother, trembling also. "The old woman told me . . . it happened before, on the night of the emigration. Her own mother had the sight."

Isobel had disappeared. She came back in a few moments with a small glass in her hand.

"Here, Mairi! Drink this, dear. No, it's not medicine; don't be silly. Brandy from the hotel."

I obeyed her and drank, and the spirit made me stagger and cough, but it brought warmth back to my frozen body. Ros was rather white-faced, but he said very little, except, "You'd better be getting home. Mairi ought to go to bed, and Jean must be quite exhausted. Uilleam Angus is just coming. I'll help Mairi down the steps to the boat."

I was glad of his arm, for I felt giddy and strange. I was still remembering fear and a flooding golden light. I was sure that Aunt Morag would die at sunset, when there was a high wind.

We were all very silent as we crossed the loch. The sky and the water were gray-black, and the lights of Alvadale swam a little in my gaze. Jean sat with her arm around me, and by the time we were approaching our own shore, I had recovered somewhat.

There were many more people than was usual on the shore at that hour, for it wasn't every day that someone came home from Glasgow. They crowded around Jean, their kindly faces eager and welcoming. Jean was rather quiet and looked very demure in her neat blue coat and plain blue hat, but when she did speak, her voice had a ring of happiness.

"Come on, Mairi!" Isobel whispered, taking my arm. "Let's run on ahead and see if the fire needs another peat and if the kettle is boiling."

When we reached the house, I sat down on my stool and looked at her.

"Isobel, what happened? Why did I say that? Why did I seem to see. . . . Do you think I really have the sight?" I believed in the power of second sight implicitly myself, and it had sounded as if Mother did, too. But Isobel came from another world, and I could read nothing in her grave face.

"I don't know, Mairi," Isobel answered slowly. "I suppose it can happen."

"Oh, it can," I said earnestly. "But I don't want it to happen to me. That other time was so very strange. Then I saw something in the past. I wasn't scared then, but it was very, very sad, and I was all alone in an—an alien crowd. The old woman said I saw the emigration that took place long ago. She believed me, but I didn't know she had told Mother." I added jerkily, "No one died then. No one was dying at all! Aunt Morag *can't* die!"

"Mairi," Isobel said, "if it should be—if you really have the sight—you must be brave about it and not let it upset you. It's more likely that Aunt Morag will soon be well again. But if what you saw is true, and you did see the future for a moment, you must try not to wonder too much. It may never happen again."

"I'll never know when it may happen," I whispered.

At that moment Mother and Jean arrived with Alan Beath, who was carrying Jean's suitcase, and in the sheer joy and relief of seeing Jean home again I grew much calmer. No one said any more about the incident on the pier, and the sharp sense of fear began to fade.

Jean took off her hat and coat and put on a big pinafore of Mother's, and there she was, just as I had always seen her in the past, moving around the living room. She caressed everything with her eyes and hands until we sat down to a very late supper.

It was quite dark by then, and we sat in the soft glow of firelight and lamplight. I saw Jean glance sadly at the old woman's chair and knew that she was missing her. But there was so much to say that we were all soon very cheerful.

That night I lay beside Jean again in the dark, and it was as if she had never been away. I was happy, deep down in my heart, but I dared not remember that in two weeks' time we must face another parting. In fact, I prayed ardently that Jean might now stay with us forever.

We awoke to clear sunshine, and the work of the house came easily. At first Mother tried to stop Jean from working, but she wouldn't listen. It was she who stirred the porridge and fried the herrings. Mother laid the table, while Isobel fed the hens and I did the milking.

Jean sang, her face radiant with happiness. Isobel sang, too, and even Mother moved around with a light step, humming softly to herself. In the midst of my own happiness I suddenly remembered that Aunt Morag was going to die on a wild golden evening. It wasn't that I was so fond of her, though she had always been kind to me. It was the fact that I seemed to know something inevitable and dreadful. If I really had that power, it made me feel very much alone.

That day Isobel was going to lunch with the Mullochs, who were spending a few weeks on Glascreagh. She had met Mr. Mulloch at the hotel one evening and he had asked her to visit them. Isobel had not seemed very eager to sample their hospitality, and when time had passed, she said the invitation must have been forgotten. Then, three days before, there had been a letter from Mrs. Mulloch.

"Oh, you must go!" I had cried. "You can tell us all about it, and if they're as awful as they sound."

Isobel had laughed and said it would be difficult to refuse.

Mrs. Mulloch was still said to hate the island *and* the islanders; she always brought her own servants with her. There was no question of employing any of the local girls, all so sorely in need of work. How often we had heard Ros mourn that the island wasn't in friendlier, more interested hands.

Isobel left early on a borrowed bicycle, wearing her smartest sweater and blue coat and skirt. By that time I was well-used to her departure into another world, but it still seemed strange that she had entry into big houses. Last year Coronallt, this year the great gray house on Glascreagh. But it was only for lunch.

The day passed peacefully when the work in the house was done. Jean and I sat in the heather on the slopes of Ulval and talked. It seemed as if I had to pour out my whole life and all the news about people we knew. I could not take my eyes off her as she sat there, slim and delicately mature, in her green cotton dress.

I told her, in confidence, all about Isobel and Colin, and how I thought she would marry him in the end. Jean nodded thoughtfully.

"I was thinking she was different, Mairi. Sometimes she has a very sad, almost puzzled look. I noticed it several times this morning, when she stopped singing. Maybe she's missing him now he's gone."

"Oh, I wish people need never go away!" I said passion-

163

ately. "Oh, Jean, I wish *you* could stay."

Jean sighed and smiled and buried her nose in the heather.

"There is no work here for me, Mairi. I have to earn my living. I—I can think of no way to stay here."

We walked over to Polleray, as arranged, and met Isobel on the rocks at three-thirty. She was brought over in one of the Mulloch boats by old Tamas MacEarn, one of the few men of the island who worked for them.

As we walked together up to Ros's house, she told us all about her visit. The Mulloch boy and girl had met her down at the harbor and taken her up to the house. She said they both attended boarding schools in England and seemed nice enough . . . much nicer than their parents. The house was very pleasant, though much too elaborately furnished.

"Heaven knows how they got the things there," she said. "It must have cost a fortune. I kept off all dangerous subjects. It would be a fine thing for Glascreagh if they did leave and someone bought the place who would do something to help."

Ros wasn't home, so we sat on a grassy bank—the same bank where Aunt Morag had spread the clothes—until he came striding over from the road. He looked very worried, but he smiled warmly at Jean.

"Well, Jean? How does it feel to be home? An almost grown-up young lady from Glasgow."

"I *am* grown-up," said Jean. "I'm seventeen now. Oh, Ros, it's wonderful!"

Isobel asked about Aunt Morag, and he looked very grave.

"She's very sick and doesn't even know me. I have just come from the hospital."

I felt sick in my stomach and cold down my spine, but that evening the clear sky dulled early to a uniform gray and there was little wind.

The next day we went down to Arbhar with Jean, so that she could visit everyone, and at noon the wind was rising. There was a great heaving on the sea, and the tide came roaring in over the skerries in the Sound. I said nothing, but I was very scared. Even at midday there was a curious yellow glow in the sky; strange, rather thick sunlight.

We stayed at Arbhar all the afternoon, and I grew more and more tense. I walked close to Jean on the way home, and she said in a low voice when we reached the house, "You look tired, Mairi. We've had a long day of visiting. What about going to bed, and I'll bring your supper to you?"

It was a relief to get indoors out of the wind and to see Mother sitting by the fire. It was only very early evening, but I was glad when Jean repeated her suggestion to Mother. I climbed into bed as soon as I had undressed and washed, and Jean brought my supper on a little tin tray. It was a great luxury to be waited on in this way, but I couldn't eat much. Fortunately there was no window in that section of the house, so the strange sunlight was hidden from me. The wind tore at the thatch, and occasionally I could hear rain beating on the windows in the living room.

"Surely the storms are not starting already?" said Mother.

Jean came and sat on the bed and began to sing, and presently Isobel came and curled up at my feet. How we sang! Those lovely, lilting airs of the Western Isles. Then Isobel started an English song she had taught me, and we were soon chorusing "Oh, no, John, no, John, no!" But all the while, as they strove to make me forget, the horror was there. The faint light that came over the partition was deep gold. It was the evening of my vision, eerie and wild.

Suddenly I sat up, wriggling my toes from under Isobel.

"I must see!" I cried. "It's no use. I have to look!"

"Don't, Mairi!" Isobel said sharply, and Jean put out her hand. But I didn't heed them. Barefooted, in my nightgown, I ran into the living room. Everywhere was gold, and the fierce wind shook the door. I opened it and looked down at the tossing, brilliant waters of the loch and the stormy sky beyond. The whole world seemed steeped in gold.

"Aunt Morag is dead!" I cried, and felt very cold and very, very sad.

I was certain that I had had the sight again, and I tried to comfort myself with what the old woman had said.

"It is a great gift. Some day it may be of help to you."

But I could not believe then that it would ever help me.

THE WEDDING
AND AFTER

Aunt Morag did die that night in September, and it
was a long time before I really got over my strange fore-
knowledge. But of course life went on, and Jean was there,
so there were plenty of things to think about.

Isobel had a letter from Colin with foreign stamps on it,
and she told us he was in Rome and was soon going on to
Sicily to paint. She was rather quiet after receiving the letter,
but she didn't seem unhappy. She was planning her novel,
which was to be about a crofting family at the turn of the
century. She asked Mother a lot of questions, and other people as well, and she was making copious notes. Jean and I
were flattered that she discussed the story with us, and,
though we couldn't remember those old days, we tried to

make suggestions. Some of them Isobel took up eagerly, and we helped very much with the names of the many characters. It was most exciting to be helping with a book again.

Ros MacBride visited us almost every evening after Aunt Morag's funeral. Probably he found his house a lonely place without the fussy little figure of his aunt. He was very attentive to Jean, but then she had always been his favorite. Sometimes they went for walks alone together, and once I saw them standing on the rocks beyond the *clachan,* so deep in talk that they seemed to have eyes for no one else.

At the end of the two weeks, Jean went back to Glasgow, dry-eyed and brave. Ros came with us to see her off, and afterward he said, with more feeling than I had ever heard in his voice, "That lass is so brave it tears at my heart. It wouldn't be so great a thing to some girls. In fact, they might welcome it as a release from boredom and lack of entertainment. But Jean belongs here with every fiber of her being. She's made of heroic stuff!"

Alas, I was certainly not made to the same pattern, for while Jean smiled gallantly and talked of next year, I had to fight with myself to hold back my tears. It was almost as bad as that first time, as far as I was concerned. But one thing comforted me. Mrs. Robertson had paid for Jean to have a berth during the night journey.

As soon as Jean was gone, it seemed, the harvest was upon us. Once more we worked all the fine hours of daylight. Of course I was in school, but I rushed home at four o'clock and joined Isobel and Mother in our own field. Then it was the *machair* again, and I always joined Isobel when I could.

The evenings were darkening, so we could not work very late. Isobel could usually find an hour or two to work on her book, and I read each chapter as it was written. On other evenings Ros walked over, and the Gaelic lessons went on. By that time Isobel could read the language quite well and was starting to write it, which she found much more difficult. Many evenings were given over entirely to Gaelic poetry, and I was always included. Isobel also continued to give me French lessons, and my desire for new knowledge burned very steadily. The future after the next summer was still dark, and no one ever discussed it in my hearing, but I began to have a deep-rooted feeling that somehow I would go on learning. It was only occasionally that I thought, with fright, that I might have to follow Jean and go into service in Glasgow or some other city.

In early November Isobel received a parcel from her publishers in London. It was copies of her book, *Hebridian Year*. That book seemed the wildest miracle to me. There was a foreword in which she acknowledged her great debt to Jean and Mairi Gilbride and to the old woman, and the book looked just the way we had imagined it on the great white shore so long ago, on that Sunday before Jean went away to Glasgow. A sea-green binding and a flight of seven wild swans picked out in silver.

Mother and I received autographed copies, and other copies were sent off to Jean, Uncle George and Colin.

Winter was upon us, and the days grew shorter and darker. Christmas approached very rapidly, and Isobel wrote more letters than usual. Around a week before the festival, several parcels and a large box that was curiously light arrived from Glasgow. When the box was opened, an artificial Christmas tree was revealed . . . its branches gleaming silver. In the box, too, were all kinds of decorations; colored glass balls and bells and many other pretty things. I hung over them, enchanted.

"You didn't do this last year," I said.

"I know, but I thought we'd decorate the place," Isobel said.

At first Mother shook her head rather reprovingly, for the charming, useless things had cost good money. But I think she loved the effect when it was finished. Isobel arranged a trail of silver stars around the statue of Our Lady on the deep window sill, and there were shining bells everywhere. The little tree stood on the table, and I loved it.

The other parcels contained presents for us, and Mother frowned again, but not for long. She never could be angry with Isobel for long. I had kept some of my "Colin money" to buy presents, especially one for Isobel. Jean helped me, and another parcel came from Glasgow, containing a pair of beautiful fur gloves, which Isobel said she would keep for special occasions.

On Christmas Eve it was calm and frosty. There was midnight Mass in the little church down by the loch, and we all walked down there under the stars. Isobel was not a Catholic, but she sometimes came with us to church. I was very happy; my only sorrow was that Jean was not with us. Once —and how long ago it seemed—she and the boys had been with us, kneeling in that tiny stone building.

It was hardly large enough, that night, to hold everyone. People had walked for miles to attend the service. The women were wrapped in shawls, and the men wore their great boots and thick jerseys. Ros was there, and Uilleam Angus and almost everyone we knew.

I was between Mother and Isobel, and soon I sank into a dream, in which the sonorous Latin rolled over my head. And suddenly, so quickly that I hadn't even time to be surprised or scared, I was in another church. It was much larger and very white, and the people were different, though the words of the Mass were the same. These people wore no shawls and great boots; they wore warm, even brightly colored clothes, and some of the women had furs. As I watched, a few more people came in, and their clothes were covered with snow. I turned slightly, and Mother was there beside me. But she no longer wore a shawl. She wore a hat and a cloth coat, and she looked fatter and very happy.

I felt serene and warm, as if I really belonged to that place. Suddenly voices soared up, singing plain chant, as the monks had done in the Benedictine Abbey at Fort Augustus in the summer. I looked over the heads in front and could see the choir. They were not monks, just ordinary people.

It passed in a flash, and I was back in the familiar church on the rocks, with Mother beside me in her shawl. There was no terror that time. If it had been a vision—a vision I did not understand—I had been happy, and I was still happy.

When the Mass was over, I walked out with the others into the frosty, starlit night, hearing the waves washing gently on the shore. The lights of Alvadale glimmered across the loch.

The next day, Christmas Day, I told Isobel.

"I think I was far away," I said. "Oh, Isobel, that time I didn't mind. What do you think it meant?"

"I don't know, Mairi," she said, but I had the strange feeling she did know. She looked almost pleased, which was strange.

January came, and school opened again. Life went on, peacefully and pleasantly enough, until almost the end of the month. Then one afternoon I came home to find Isobel out and Mother standing uncertainly by the hearth. She had a most unusual look of excitement and joy on her face.

"What is it?" I asked, staring at her. Her eyes were wet, but the happiness was unmistakable.

"Oh, Mairi, Ros has been here," said Mother. "He talked to me. . . . Oh, I had hoped for this, but thought I might be wrong."

"What?" I asked sharply, much-puzzled.

"Why. . . . Oh, indeed, it will be a wonderful thing! He wants to go to Glasgow and ask Jean to marry him."

"Marry Jean?" I was so astonished that I could hardly speak. "But—but I know he likes Jean, but she is so young, and Ros . . . Ros is *old*."

"He is not thirty yet. He says it was always Jean, but he was waiting until she grew up. He is a very good man, and a clever man, and Jean. . . . I have the feeling that she does love him. When she came home, I knew that she was a woman at heart. And I was only seventeen myself when I married your father."

I sat down with a bump on my stool. The idea of Jean married was hard to grasp, but almost at once I saw the incredible joy in the idea. If Jean married Ros, she would live on the island again and she would never have to go away. Jean and Ros . . . the idea had never once occurred to me, but I suddenly wondered if Isobel had known. She had said something about Ros having a secret.

Mother and I talked for a long time, and Isobel came home to find no meal ready and the fire only dully smoldering. When she heard the news, she was thrilled and eager, but I thought not surprised.

"Did you know?" I asked, in a low voice, as we prepared the supper.

"Well, in a way," she murmured back. "He never quite

said. . . . But I was sure it was Jean. Why do you think he came so often? To hear news of her, to read her letters."

"I thought he came to see you," I said. "I told you. I did so want. . . . But there was Colin. Oh, Isobel, do you think Jean will marry him?"

"I'm sure she will," said Isobel. "You saw them together. Jean's young, but she's a born homemaker. The age difference doesn't matter. You should be very happy, Mairi."

"I *am* happy," I said, but I hadn't really got over the shock.

In a few days Ros crossed the stormy Minch, and eventually a telegram came from Glasgow. It said simply: "All well. Love, Ros and Jean." So we knew that they would be married.

Eventually Ros returned alone, for of course Jean could not leave Mrs. Robertson at once. She was to come home early in March to prepare for the wedding.

The days passed very quickly; the short gray winter days when the Isles were swept by gales and drenched in cold rain. Breakfast by lamplight and then down to the school in the faint light. Lessons and meals and the warm hearth . . . the clacking sound of Isobel's typewriter, Ros's great knock on the door, the crash of waves on the shore, and the beating of wild swans' wings.

At times the north wind brought frost and dry, bright weather to the Isles. Then the loch shone and the solan geese rose and cried over the silvered *peat-hags*. On Saturdays and Sundays like that, Isobel left her book and we went out for the whole of the daylight. I borrowed Maggie Campbell's bicycle, and by that time Isobel had bought her own. Together we traveled through the icy, silent air over the long, rough island roads. We went to the shores of the northern sea lochs and, leaving our bicycles somewhere in the brown desolation, climbed up into the hills, gray-white with frost and bound in a breathless silence. Standing on the summits of the hills, we could see long distances to the islands further north. Once I said, "I wish I could visit them all. I'd like to go to the most northerly island . . . that's North Rona, I think."

Isobel was standing on the rock beside me, her face glowing in the cold air.

"If ever I have a daughter," she said slowly, "I shall call her Rona. It will remind me of the Isles whenever I say it."

At once some of my happiness fled. Isobel had been with us nearly two years, but I knew that time was running out. Jean was coming back, but probably Isobel would soon go away. The winter, she had said, and soon it would be spring.

"Are you going to marry Colin?" I asked. We had hardly mentioned the subject for months; but I felt she was my friend, and a friend could ask, surely?

Isobel turned, and we began to tramp down the hill. Her face was grave and thoughtful.

"I think so, Mairi, if he still wants it when we meet again."

"But when will you meet?"

"In the spring, when he comes back from Italy." Suddenly she smiled. "I *think* he still wants it. He mentions it in every letter."

"Then I'll never see you again," I whispered, and at that she put her arm around me.

"Never see me again? Don't be a goose! I don't give up my dearest friends that easily. Wherever I am—wherever *you* are—we'll meet sometimes."

"I suppose *I* shall still be in Glen Gaoth," I said, and then

174

I added quickly, "Oh, Isobel, sometimes I long so much to see other places. Glasgow and London and Italy. I'll always belong to the Isles and want to come home, but sometimes I feel so restless."

When Isobel answered all she said was, "Who can say?" I didn't find it a very satisfactory answer.

In early March Ros went to Glasgow to bring Jean home. It was a very cold night when they were expected back, brilliantly starry and with a touch of frost. Mother wouldn't hear of my crossing the loch so late, because I had had a slight cold, so I stood at the door, muffled in shawls and feeling sick with excitement.

When Jean came, she looked fatter than she had in the autumn and a good deal older. She was our Jean still, but happier, more radiant. The thin little girl in the shabby coat who had sailed away nearly two years earlier seemed very far in the past. She wore a dark red dress that was very simple and well cut, and her smooth brown hair had a healthy shine on it. On her left hand sparkled Ros's engagement ring.

We all sat around the fire for hours, though it was very late when they arrived. Isobel had insisted on ordering a box of delicacies from Glasgow, and we feasted wonderfully in the lamplight. I sat on my little stool, leaning against Jean's knees. I felt that I loved Ros, as I looked up at his kindly, clever face. He had brought Jean back to us.

Isobel was laughing and almost as radiant as Jean. Her moods in those days were more varied than they had once been. She had put on a new emerald-green dress for the occasion, and her soft, bright hair was bound with an emerald ribbon.

I can see it all so clearly now. The glow of the fire on the dear, familiar faces, and the look of peace in Mother's fine, tired eyes.

Ros went at last, back to his cold, empty house, but the rest of us sat on for a while longer, discussing the wedding, which was to take place during the second week in April.

Isobel was going to visit her stepmother toward the end of March and then go on to London for a few days, but she said that of course she would be back for the wedding. Meanwhile she helped Jean all she could. In the daytime they were often over at Ros's house, cleaning and planning and even doing some painting and decorating, with which Ros helped. Then, night after night, we all worked at Jean's trousseau to the sound of hail and thunder. Jean always seemed to be singing. The sight of her fuller, rosy cheeks and eager, happy eyes sometimes made me catch my breath with almost unbearable pleasure. I think that my love for Jean was without doubt the strongest emotion of my youth. I loved her because I needed her, but I loved her enough to rejoice in her happiness.

Yet things changed in a mysterious way before Isobel took her departure. Jean was suddenly more serious, more thoughtful, and several times she and Mother broke off conversations when I appeared. Mother hardly ever wrote letters, but then she wrote several and didn't give them to me to mail, and twice she went over the loch to the bank.

"Are you worried about money?" I asked anxiously. "Oh, Mother, I thought we'd saved a bit. I know we'll miss Isobel's money if she goes, but when I leave school I'll help you on the croft. If—that is, if I don't have to go away and work."

And Mother hugged me and said there was nothing to

worry about, but didn't explain.

I was left with a feeling of vague disquiet; but what with school and helping Jean, there wasn't much time for thinking.

Isobel left on a cold, wild night, taking her finished novel with her. She wrote from Gloucestershire and then from London. In London she met Colin again, as I had somehow known she would. She said he had had a wonderful time painting in Italy, and *Crofter's Child* had been accepted for the Royal Academy. By the same mail there was a large, flat parcel for me, and to my amazement it was from Colin. A photograph of the picture, with his huge, scrawling signature on the back.

Ros and Jean were married in the little church down by the loch on a bright April day. Isobel returned the night before, bringing a bouquet of daffodils and white narcissus, still miraculously fresh, and some lovely things from London; cushion covers and tablecloths in rich, gay colors that filled our drab little room with brilliance. Jean clung to her for a moment, in sheer inarticulate happiness and gratitude, then crouched in rapture over the beautiful things.

It was the daffodils that held me in a curious, still ecstasy. I had heard so often from Isobel about English parkland and orchards scattered with daffodils, but I had never imagined them in our house, golden and glowing.

Jean was married in a dress and coat of soft, bright brown that showed up her pink cheeks and the gloss of her hair. And she wore a little yellow hat that was almost the color of the daffodils. Isobel had made me a new dress for the occasion, and I was so excited by the whole thing that I spent an almost sleepless night.

Oh, how vividly I remember that morning when Father

177

Donald married Ros and Jean in the familiar little church on the rocks. All our friends were there, and afterward so many people crowded into our house that we could hardly breathe. They all stayed there until late in the evening, long after Ros and Jean had set off on foot for Polleray. Isobel and I had slipped away on bicycles in the late afternoon to light fires and make everything ready for their homecoming.

That night was a real *ceilidh,* for how we sang and how we talked, and never a word of English. The peat and tobacco smoke hung thickly in the air, and all the food we had prepared disappeared.

Sometimes, as the laughter and talk went on, I thought of Ros and Jean alone in the house within sound of the Atlantic Ocean, and I felt a little desolate because, soon, Mother and I might be alone. Yet I was glad that Jean was happy and would never be an exile again.

The next morning, of course, seemed a terrible anticlimax. It was the Easter holidays, so I didn't have to go to school. Mother and Isobel both seemed unusually quiet as we did the work of the house, and I was glad when Isobel said, "It's a beautiful day, Mairi. Go and see if you can borrow Maggie Campbell's bicycle and we'll take a picnic and go out for the day."

The sun had a touch of warmth in it, and it was good to be out. We cycled all around the long arms of the loch and away north toward Coronallt. When we were still some miles away, we could see the big house on the brown slopes.

"The Carlows are there," said Isobel. "They were on the steamer the night I returned."

"The absentee English landlords," I said, quoting Ros. The Carlows owned the whole island, but were hardly ever there, and Lord Carlow seemed to take little interest in any of the problems.

We sat in a sheltered hollow to eat our lunch. The snow was still gleaming on the higher hills, but it was almost warm by a tumbling burn. Isobel was very silent until she had eaten the last crumb, then she turned to me suddenly.

"Mairi, I have something to tell you. Your mother asked me to. She said it might come better from me."

"What?" I asked, in fright, for her face and tone were grave.

"I'm afraid it may be a shock, but it had to come, Mairi. In the first place, dear, I'm going to marry Colin in the late summer, probably in London."

I turned to her, still shaken and anxious, for I felt there was much more to come.

"Oh! Oh, I do hope you will be happy."

"I hope we will be. Now, Mairi, listen very carefully. You're going to have a choice. Nothing is absolutely fixed. You wondered why Martin didn't send money home, didn't you? Well, he didn't send it because he was saving it, in case your mother and you wanted to go to Canada. For your fares and to furnish an apartment. And your mother does want to go now." I jerked and gasped, and she said, "Wait! She can't keep on working as hard as she does, Mairi; and Martin says he can find her a well-paid and easy job looking after an old lady he knows. Just in the daytime. And if you went, too, you could go to a good school and keep on with your education. But you don't *have* to go. Ros and Jean would love to have you go to live with them. Ros says he would write to friends at Glasgow University and ask them to send you books and a plan of work, and maybe, later, you could go over to the mainland to take exams." Her hand had come out to hold mine tightly. "Oh, Mairi, don't look like that!"

I stared at the sunlit scene, but hardly saw it. It was as if I hadn't known I was dying and now I did know. I had been living perhaps my last weeks in the croft-house in Glen Gaoth . . . the last weeks, anyway, of peace and a kind of security. Yet I had known that the hard outdoor work was making Mother terribly tired; I had known that Isobel would go and that my own future was uncertain.

But this . . . Mother definitely going to Canada and the chance for me to go, too. Away from the island, as the boys had gone, to a far, distant country.

Isobel went on talking quietly.

"Ros's health is splendid now, Mairi. In two or three years, whether you stay with them or go on ahead, he may go back to his college lecturing. He and Jean may decide to go to Canada for a time. I think Jean will be happy to agree; in spite of loving the island."

Changes. . . . Oh, changes! I sprang up, dashing sudden tears from my eyes.

"Don't come, Isobel! I—I have to think!" And I stumbled down the hillside, seized my bicycle and rode off at breakneck speed along the narrow, rough road. There were many bends, and I didn't even hear the car coming. It was almost upon me before I swerved, screamed and fell. I thought, as I felt sharp pain, "I'm dead! I shan't have to choose!" and then everything went black.

MAIRI'S CHOICE

I wasn't dead, but I didn't open my eyes for some time. Before that, though, I had been aware of voices . . . anxious, unfamiliar voices, and then I heard Isobel say, "She's waking up! I think she's only bumped and bruised, and something's wrong with her ankle."

I saw her face close above me and was aware that I was lying on something deliciously soft. Then I looked beyond her to a pink, pretty room; the most attractive room I had ever seen in all my life. Near the door stood a big man with a red face and a plump, middle-aged woman wearing a smart green dress.

When I struggled to sit up, Isobel put her hand gently over me and held me down.

"The doctor's coming, Mairi. Just lie still. You're all right, dear."

"But where *am* I?"

"At Coronallt. You rode almost straight into a car that Lord Carlow was driving."

At Coronallt! That house that loomed in a vague way over all our lives. I gasped and lay still and heard Isobel say to the two by the door that she would stay with me until the doctor arrived and that she wouldn't let me talk until he had examined me.

The doctor came almost at once. He was not the one I knew, but the other doctor who looked after the whole north of the island. He soon said there was nothing much wrong with me, except cuts and bruises and a badly sprained ankle. And of course shock.

"She ought not to be moved for a few days," he said to the woman in the green dress, who was in the room again.

"But of course not. We'll look after her. Miss Darroch can be sent home in the car, and the chauffeur will bring the child's mother back. She'll want to see for herself."

At that I came completely to myself. I was so anxious to make myself clear that I wasn't even shy of Lady Carlow.

"Thank you very much," I said, in the good English I had picked up from Isobel. "But Isobel will tell my mother I'm all right. I—I don't want her to come, please. She is very busy and tired, and I—I have to think before I see her."

"Well, don't think too hard for the moment," the doctor said. I noticed that none of them seemed surprised, so maybe Isobel had explained in private.

She said she had, when we were alone before she left.

"They're kind enough people, Mairi, though perhaps a bit stupid by Ros's standards. Lord Carlow thought he'd killed

182

you, though it wouldn't have been his fault, poor man, if he had. Let them be nice to you, and think if you *must*."

"If—if only I'd known," I whispered. "Mother must have been planning this for a long time. I was old enough to be told."

"I think she had some vague intention of going from the time the boys left. That was probably why she let you come to the mainland and learn French and all the rest. But she didn't make up her mind until she heard about Jean and Ros. I told her you ought to be told, but she wanted you to enjoy the wedding. It will all work out, Mairi. I think you'll be strong and brave."

I didn't feel either strong or brave when Isobel had gone away and left me in the pink room at Coronallt Lodge. Yet one side of me was awed and fascinated. A young English maid brought me a tea tray, with a little rosy teapot and a milk jug, cup, saucer and plate to match. There was thin bread and butter and several delicious creamy cakes.

"It's all so pretty," I said shyly. I was much shyer with her than I had been with Lady Carlow. "I love this room."

"It's Miss Joanna's room when she's here," she said. "Their youngest daughter."

So they hadn't put me in the servants' quarters! They were even, it turned out, going to lend me Miss Joanna's clothes. Nightdresses and pink fluffy slippers and a padded silk robe.

Such luxury! It wasn't right, of course, as we had always thought, that some people should have so much and the crofters so little, but they did seem quite kind . . . not the indifferent ogres I had pictured.

My cuts and bruises hurt and so did my ankle, and, when twilight began to fall, my heart hurt, too. Because I had to make a great decision. How could I let Mother cross the ocean without me? But would I have the courage to start life again in a new country, without Jean and Ros and Isobel? There would be Martin, of course, and Margaret and the baby.

Lord Carlow found me in the half-dark and switched on a pink-shaded light. I blinked and tried to hide my tears. He stood by the bed, red-faced and large, wearing a dinner jacket . . . the first I had ever seen.

"You mustn't lie in the dark and be miserable," he said. "Look! There are plenty of books. I'll pass you some. What do you like? Story books . . . school stories. . . ."

"I would like real novels, please," I said, with dignity, and he laughed.

"Miss Darroch said you were clever. Probably got more brains in your little finger than I have all over, eh? And you've a problem, she said. You were riding that bicycle like a mad thing because you'd just heard you might be going to live in Canada."

"Or stay here," I whispered, "with my sister and—and her husband. But my mother's going. I—I don't know which to choose." Then I added in a burst, "There is nothing here for any of us. But the island is my home. No work and little houses. . . ." I realized with horror that the words weren't very tactful, when I was lying in his big house and eating his food.

He sighed and took a turn around the room.

"I know conditions are bad. Some say hard things about us, don't they? Wish I'd never bought the island. Too big a problem for me. But Canada is a fine country, you know. Miss Darroch said your brother is doing well. You could come back some day . . . study to be a doctor or a nurse. Or even a politician," he added. "Women are on the up and up, aren't they? Especially brainy ones. You go to Canada, but come back when you're ready."

So it was the absentee English landlord, the ogre, who

helped me to choose, but there was something else, too. I tossed in pain almost all that night, thinking over his words. I wasn't quite sure what a politician was; something to do with the government, I thought. Those people in London who were usually so indifferent to Scottish problems.

And, sometime during the night, I remembered my Christmas "vision." Had I seen myself in Canada? If I had, then I had been happy, and so was Mother.

Realization was so wonderful, so joyful, that I quite forgot the pain in my foot. For this was what the old woman must have meant. Maybe she had had a touch of the sight herself. That third vision must have been sent to help me, in this time of decision.

I had really had no doubt that I would have to go to Canada with Mother, but now I knew for certain that we would be happy there. That Mother would wear good clothes and we would one day be together in that other church.

It would be terrible to leave my island, and Ros and Jean and Isobel, but I was sure that I would see them again. I would have to have faith in the future.

Thinking thus, I fell asleep.

I was at Coronallt for nearly a week. The Carlows didn't seem in any hurry to send me home. When I could walk fairly well, I explored the big house or sat reading in the housekeeper's room. But when Isobel came to see me, as she did twice, we had tea in the drawing room, with Lord and Lady Carlow and the middle-aged married couple who were the only other guests.

I told Isobel that I had decided to go to Canada and repeated what Lord Carlow had said. I felt quite calm about it by then, though sometimes the pain of leaving gripped me. And other times I felt overwhelming excitement because we would go on a great ship across the ocean.

"But when will we go?" I asked her, the second time she came.

"At the end of June, Mairi. That's what your mother has written to tell Martin. And he'll make the reservations and fix it all. I'll go to Glasgow with you and see you both on the ship."

My face crumpled at the thought of that parting, and she added quickly, "Colin and I may come to see you in a year or two. He can go and paint in the Rockies or somewhere, and I'll stay with you."

So, with hopes and fears and plans, I went home . . . back to Mother and Ruari and Isobel and the work of each day. The weeks passed, and everything was fixed. Ruari was going to Jean, and our croft was to be taken over by a young couple recently married.

I won't write much about those last days; in fact, I can't even now. Especially I can't tell about that undarkening June night when we sailed out of Loch Alvadale, after the parting with Ros and Jean and all our friends. The air was quiet, and the peat smoke rose up straight; dogs barked far away in the hills. I stood alone, staring back at the island until it had quite disappeared.

That was six years ago, and now I am a Canadian girl, but I still mean to go back to the Isles. I am going to be a teacher, and some day I shall go and work on one of the larger islands. I shall start that way, but I'll take part in island affairs and work—oh, how I will work—to make things better.

In college I have met a Scottish boy who was brought to Canada as a small child. He, too, wants to go back. We are not engaged yet, but I have a feeling we may go together.

Mother is very well and seems happy. She looks quite different from the thin, worn-faced woman in a rough, thick shawl. We haven't very much money, but we are comfortable; Martin is part-owner of a garage now, and he helps. Neill is still farming in Alberta, and we saw him last year.

Jean and Ros live in Toronto and have two sons. They stayed on at Polleray for nearly three years. Long before they left, Colin sold his properties in Rossshire and Wales and bought Glascreagh Island. Isobel wrote me that Colin said he would be another absentee landlord, since he didn't feel he would ever stay in one place for long. But he at once began to work on improvements, and they always employ local labor in Glascreagh House. Isobel's daughter Rona was born there, and I was so happy to hear that.

If ever *I* have a daughter, I think I would like her to be born in the Isles, even if she comes to Canada later. Sometimes I think of that time when I had to make a choice. If I had chosen the other way and stayed in Scotland with Ros and Jean, I would have been almost seventeen by the time they decided to emigrate. I might even have fallen in love with a young crofter, and my life would have been very different.

Isobel and Rona stayed with us for six weeks last summer, while Colin made a painting trip into the mountains. Isobel hadn't really altered at all, and she still writes books. It was so lovely to have her with us again, and to hear her singing as she helped with the housework. But she didn't sing the "Glascreagh Love Lilt." Maybe she knew I couldn't bear it because of the memories it would start.

And then I heard it as I went down the stairs, and so I wrote this book. I lived again those early years of my life, and, while I wrote, I was back there on that island thousands of miles away . . . my island in a green sea.

Gaelic Glossary

It is rather difficult to give Gaelic pronunciations phonetically, but these suggestions will give the reader some idea. "Ch," as in "lochan," is always guttural and never pronounced as "k"; "bh" or "mh" in the middle of a word is usually sounded like "v," but occasionally not sounded at all.

Pronunciation, or even the language itself, can vary slightly in different districts.

Arbhar. Pronounced Ar-var.

Beannachd leat. An old Gaelic blessing. Pro. B-yen-uchk leht.

Caileag. Little girl. Pro. Kal-ak.

Cailleach. Old woman. Pro. Kyl-lach.

Ceilidh. A gathering for songs and stories. Pro. Kay-lee.

Cairistiona. Christina. Pronounced more or less the same.

Ceit. Kate. Pronounced Kate.

Clachan. A very small village. Pro. Clach-an.

Crofting. Farming. Usually in a very small way. Not a Gaelic word.

Eisd! Listen! Pro. more or less like East.

Fraoch. Heather. Pro. Fra-och.

Glascreagh. Pro. Glas-cray-eh.

Gaoth. Wind. Pro. with a hard G.

Lochan. A very small lake, usually with reeds and water lilies. Pro. Loch-an.

Machair. Grazing and arable land on the western seaboard of the islands. Pro. Mach-ar.

Mairi. Mary. But pronounced more like the French Marie.

Mo chridhe. My heart. Pro. Mo cree.

Mo thruaigh! My trouble! Pro. Mo throu-eye.

Muireall. Muriel. Pronounced the same.

Peat-hags. Wet and peaty moorland.

Sound of Sleat. Pro. Slate.

Sorcha. Clara. Pro. Sor-cha.

Tangle and (sea) *wrack.* Both seaweed of various kinds. Not exclusively Gaelic words.

Tir-nan-Og. The Land of the Ever-Young. Pro. Cheer-nun-Awk.

Uilleam. William. Pro. the same.